COLLECTION OF BRITISH AUTHORS TAUCHNITZ EDITION. VOL. 3791; THE GREEN EYE OF GOONA; STORIES OF A CASE OF TOKAY

Published @ 2017 Trieste Publishing Pty Ltd

ISBN 9780649597567

Collection of British Authors Tauchnitz Edition. Vol. 3791; The Green Eye of Goona; Stories of a
Case of Tokay by Arthur Morrison

Edited by Trieste Publishing Pty Ltd.
Cover @ 2017

www.triestepublishing.com

ARTHUR MORRISON

COLLECTION OF BRITISH AUTHORS TAUCHNITZ EDITION. VOL. 3791; THE GREEN EYE OF GOONA; STORIES OF A CASE OF TOKAY

Trieste

COLLECTION

OF

BRITISH AUTHORS

TAUCHNITZ EDITION.

VOL. 3791.

THE GREEN EYE OF GOONA.

BY

ARTHUR MORRISON.

IN ONE VOLUME.

TAUCHNITZ EDITION.

By the same Author,

THE

GREEN EYE OF GOONA

STORIES OF A CASE OF TOKAY

BY

ARTHUR MORRISON

AUTHOR OF

"TALES OF MEAN STREETS," "THE HOLE IN THE WALL," ETC.

COPYRIGHT EDITION

LEIPZIG

BERNHARD TAUCHNITZ

1905.

CONTENTS.

THE GREEN EYE OF GOONA.

I.

THE FIRST MAGNUM.

I.

THE year 1902 drew to a close, and Delhi was swarming thrice its common size in preparation for the Great Durbar, whereat the accession of the first English Emperor of India was to be proclaimed. Northward, beyond the historic Ridge, a new and an even more wonderful Delhi had sprung up in the course of weeks; a Delhi of ten thousand tents, with more than thirty miles of streets between them; a city that it would take a man seven or eight hours of continuous smart marching to walk round.

For weeks the tramp of elephants and horses had

filled the air day by day, and had rarely ceased at
night.   The camps of the native princes lay in carefully planned order, and the comings and goings of the
princes themselves—emulous, proud, jealous, in trifles
—were announced punctiliously by the proper number
of guns, from twenty-one downward, the envied and
eagerly sought salute that grades Indian princes by
absolute mathematical scale.

Under the frail canvas of that camp lay the ransom
of a hundred kings in gems and gold and precious
stuffs.   Diamonds, emeralds, rubies, pearls, in strings,
in dozens and in scores, each stone a marvel even
among the rest, were brought together there in an as-
semblage impossible to make in any other part of the
globe.   Even the lesser rajahs, thakores, and nawabs
had brought for their adornment many gems of great
name, such as singly would stand heirlooms in the royal
houses of Europe.

Not the least renowned among these was the Eye
of Deccan, the wonderful green diamond belonging to
the Rajah of Goona.   Indeed, amid that assembly of
marvellous gems the Eye of Deccan took rank among
the very greatest—far higher rank than the Rajah took

among the princes; for he could claim only a nine-gun salute, which placed him merely in the seventh grade, with the eleven-gun, the thirteen-gun, the fifteen-gun, the seventeen-gun, and the nineteen-gun degrees between it and the topmost rank of twenty-one guns, reserved for the greatest three native princes of all India.

The Eye of Deccan was the more ancient name of the jewel, which nowadays was more commonly called the Eye of Goona. It was famous alike for its colour, its size, and its history. Of coloured diamonds the green are the rarest, and this was not only of a gloriously brilliant emerald tint, but of extraordinary size, being of nearly three times the weight of the renowned pale-green diamond kept at Dresden, as well as of incomparably finer colour. In shape it was an oval brilliant fully an inch and a half long and a shade more than an inch wide. When this amazing stone had left the mine no man could tell, for it had been known all over India as the envy and contention of kings for nearly a thousand years. Purchase, spoliation, murder, treachery, theft, and war had passed it from hand to hand till at last it had rested in the treasure-house of Akbar the Great, and there remained till the death of

his descendant Aurungzebe.   In the fall of the dynasty
of Akbar early in the eighteenth century and the
general disruption which followed it, the Eye of Deccan
vanished, and it was only on the establishment of safe
and steady government under British domination that
it was allowed to reappear—this time in possession of
the Rajah of Goona, ancester of the present Rajah, now
camping at Delhi to do homage to the new Emperor
represented by his Viceroy.

One after another through the last weeks of the
year the trumpeting, trampling processions rolled into
camp till the tents were full of princes and their
retinues; and then, when the bustle of constant arrivals
had begun to slacken, on a cool, clear night, the
customary noises of tethered elephants and waking
horses were broken upon by a riot of human shouts
and yells.

The disturbance was over in a very few minutes,
and the rumour ran round the camp that a thief had
entered the tents of the Rajah of Goona, and had been
cut down by the Rajah's Chief Minister as he was
crawling away.   And in the morning more was known.
The thief was dead, and his body, black, naked, and

oiled from top to toe, had been identified; he was a thief by trade, of a family of thieves. He had entered the tent in the dead of night, had effected his robbery, and was escaping silently, when he was observed by Mehta Singh, the Chief Minister, and cut down, two blows of a heavy tulwar putting an end to his thieving for all time. And the plunder which he was carrying away was no other than the Eye of Goona itself!

This last news kept the camp talking from end to end. The audacity of the thief was great enough, but the wonder was how, having entered the tent without being seen by the guards, he was able to put his hand directly on the great jewel, or to pick the lock of the case in which it was doubtless kept. The thing carried a smell of treachery; it seemed clear that somebody in the Rajah's train had betrayed his trust and sold information to the thief. This was agreed on all hands; but at any rate the plot had been frustrated, and by the faithful vigilance of Mehta Singh the jewel had been restored; that was enough. More, the great ceremony was now coming on, so the camp turned to the business before it, and talked little more of the attempt on the Eye of Goona.

Talked little of it, that is to say, till after the great
Durbar—even later.   For it was not till the whole programme of the splendid fortnight had been worked through,
and the Viceroy had departed in state, that the rumour
—the news, for it was proclaimed a certainty—hummed
through the breaking camp that the stone which had
been taken from the hands of the dead thief was now
found to be a mere coloured crystal, and that the **Eye
of Goona** was gone after all!

Brought out into the light of day amid other great
jewels, the supposed Eye had seemed curiously dull
and lacking in fire.   The Rajah grew suspicious, and
when opportunity served he sent for his own lapidary,
who condemned the imposture at sight.

"What did it mean?   At first it seemed probable
that there must have been two thieves, with a plan to
substitute the imitation stone for the real; that they
had been interrupted in the very act of the robbery,
and that one had escaped in the darkness with the
jewel, while the other had been pounced on by Mehta
Singh before he had "planted" the imitation.   But
then another and a simpler possibility grew apparent.

Might not the Eye of Goona have been stolen already, before the Rajah's train came to Delhi, and the imitation left in its place? It might have been months before—even years; and while the slain thief had lost his life in an unwitting attempt to steal the sham gem, the real jewel might lie safely in the hands of another.

Of the two possibilities this last seemed the more likely, and grew into more general acceptance as the efforts of the police and of the Rajah's secret agents proved futile. The camps broke up and scattered throughout India, carrying with them to every corner the news of the loss of the Eye of Deccan.

Bazaar rumour said this and that, telling lies and truth in good admixture. And at last there came in whispers a strange tale, told now in one way and then in another; but the substance of it was that there was no more Mehta Singh in Goona. Dark things are done in the smaller native states, which the British Residents hear less of than is whispered in the vernacular in the streets. Mehta Singh had vanished, that all the whisperers agreed; but how he had vanished was a matter of doubt and mystery. It would have been no new or strange thing for a rajah in his own palace,

enraged at the loss of a favourite jewel, to take
vengeance on the officer whose duty it had been to
keep it safe, or who had failed to recover it, once it
had gone, no matter how faithfully he had tried; and
such a thing would be done with secrecy and hidden
with great care in these days of the British *Raj*. The
same fate might have befallen any member of the
household suspected of complicity in the theft. However that might be, the fate of Mehta Singh, who had
struck down the thief in the Durbar camp, remained as
much a mystery as that of the Eye of Goona itself.

II.

AMONG the many Europeans attracted to the great
spectacle at Delhi were a good few who came on business. There were travellers from firms in Europe and
in Calcutta, as well as many traders on their own
account. For instance, there was Hahn, of Europe in
general, who bought and sold all over the world whatever was to be bought cheap and sold dear, from old
Italian masters to domestic machinery. Hahn spoke

English for the most part, and called himself Frank, though there were those who called him Franz, and there was a trifling accent in his excellent English that seemed to give them reason; but others held that neither Frank nor Franz nor Hahn were names he had always used, and that his first sally upon the commercial world had been from Galicia. Hahn had effected a trade here and there, had sold on his own account and on commission some sporting guns among the rajahs, and some new European furniture: and he had picked up a curious bargain in the shape of a dozen magnums of old Tokay, which had been lying forgotten in some great Delhi cellar since early in the nineteenth century; and in the middle of the celebrations he had been laid up with a bad touch of fever. It was while he had been so laid up that he sent to beg a call from Mr. Harvey Crook, who was himself a visitor on business.

Harvey Crook was not what one would call a dealer, although it was a fact that he made his living by deals in strange things—deals few and far between, but each sufficiently profitable to keep him going in the way of life he loved best, travelling the world through, and taking adventures as they came. He was a wiry man of about the middle size or a trifle under, dark because of his constant travel, though naturally of the complexion of the average Englishman; keen of eye and active as a cat; and his age was thirty-five.

He received Hahn's message with some surprise, for his acquaintance with the man was very slight. But on reflection he could not remember that anybody else about Delhi just then was any more intimate with Hahn than he was himself; so with no particular enthusiasm, he lit another cigar and strolled into the Delhi streets.

He found the dealer lying in a darkened room, in a house which had been hired temporarily as an annexe to a hotel. There was not much sickness about, it was an uncommon time of year for fever, and Crook wondered to find the room kept so dark unless the case were very bad indeed. It scarcely seemed that it was, for Hahn greeted him with great friendliness.

"Good day, my dear Crook," he said; "you are an angel of light here in the dark room. It is good of you to come." There was a faint likeness to "goot" and "gom" in two of the words, and "angel" sounded a little like "anchel," but not enough to notice.

"Not at all," Crook replied civilly. "What can I do for you? Not very bad, I hope? Wrong time of year for fever isn't it?"

"Yes, yes, but I am very subject. I am better now —just for an hour. I take it like that; presently I shall be much worse. When will you be going back home? Soon, I expect?"

"Yes—the next boat from Bombay when the shindy's over. It's lucky my passage was booked—they're pretty well crowded up."

"That's the *Rajapur,* isn't it? Not a mail-boat?"

"Quite right. The P. & O. mail's a week after. The *Rajapur's* a slower boat, but all I could get, and quite good enough. Want me to do anything for you aboard?"

Harvey Crook was sitting by the bed, and Hahn took him by the wrist. "I want you to take a case," he said, "a case of wine. Will you? I'll do as much for you some day. It's valuable stuff."

Harvey Crook's home-going baggage was small enough, for he was carrying almost nothing but his personal belongings. "All right," he said. "I daresay I can. Want me to take it to a customer at home?"

"No, no—not to a customer; only to take it and see it isn't damaged. If you will, of course I'll pay expenses, and I'm good for a commission when the stuff's sold. I don't see why I shouldn't get a hundred for it if I wait a bit. It's a dozen magnums of Imperial Tokay—eighty years in bottle! It's been lying lost for three-quarters of a century, and I picked it up for next to nothing, on a deal for something else. No doubt it was part of some present—perhaps to the old Mogul. You'll take it for me, won't you?"

"Oh yes, I'll take it. But what shall I do with it when I get it home? I shan't be wanting to sit still, you know."

"Thank you, thank you, my dear Crook—that will be all right. If I don't let you know before you start I will by the time you reach England—the mail will be some days ahead of you, of course, though it starts a week later; and if necessary I'll cable. You shall hear from me as soon as you arrive, somehow. You may be assured, my dear Crook, that it shan't hamper you in the least—not in the least; I should like to get it off my mind at once. Will you take it with you now?"

"Yes, if you like. Where is it? I'll get an *ekka.*"

"Will you? There's a good chap. I wouldn't trouble you, but there's nobody I can trust, you know —I wouldn't ask any of them rascally Germans." Here again the word was a little like "Chermance," but only a very little. "I thought to myself," Hahn went on, "that I'd ask you to do it, if you didn't mind, being a man I'd trust with anything, of course, my dear Crook."

"All right," Crook answered, with an embarrassed laugh. "Not that I've met a great many people who say that!"

"Ah, but I know I could trust you anywhere, my dear Crook," the other went on, with his eyes intently on the younger man's face; for Hahn was a man of very near fifty, with a short grey beard. "I knew I could trust you, especially as you know it's an important thing for me, with a wife and family at home. Things have been very bad lately, and a clear hundred pounds—if I can get as much—or even eighty or ninety would mean a good deal more to me than you might think. Where will you stay in London?"

"At Standish's Hotel. Letters will find me either there or at the Aborigine Club."

2*

"Thank you, thank you ever so much, my dear Crook," concluded Hahn, gripping Crook's hand with fervour. "Have they got your *ekka?* I won't keep you any longer—so good of you to come and all. Good-bye! They will be bringing my medicine. Good-bye! You'll be sure to take particular care none of the bottles are broken, won't you? That would be terrible —spoil the dozen—and it's one of the reasons I'm asking you to do it, care being so important, you know. Good-bye!"

Harvey Crook went off a little amused. Hahn was a thrifty soul, and had made an enormous great fuss about eighty or a hundred pounds' worth of old wine; no doubt a sick man's fancy had something to do with the matter. As for things having been bad with Hahn of late, that seemed very unlikely. But, of course, he reflected, a wife and family must make a good deal of difference; though—no doubt owing to his slight acquaintance—he had never heard of Hahn's wife and family before.

III.

THE voyage home on the *Rajapur* was pleasant enough, the cooler season making its influence felt to some extent even in the Red Sea. Among Harvey Crook's fellow-passengers he came much in contact with Mr. Lyman W. Merrick, a wealthy American and a very good fellow, who was taking his first holiday for many years in the shape of a tour round the world with his daughter, Daisy, and, of course, had made the Delhi Durbar his chief objective. Harvey Crook's many tales of his experiences by land and sea vastly entertained Mr. Merrick, and went all the way to reconcile him to the necessity, repugnant to his habits of "hustle," of travelling in a slower vessel than the mail-ship because of the impossibility of obtaining berths in anything faster.

"Well, Mr. Crook," said the American as they sat smoking on deck-chairs on an early day of the voyage, "Mr. Henry Crook, I believe?" Mr. Merrick paused, for there chanced to be two Crooks aboard.

"Not Henry—Harvey Crook's my name. That other passenger is Mr. Henry Crook—a stranger to me; the stout man, I mean."

"Ah—jesso. Well, say, Mr. Harvey Crook, you've had a pretty advent'rous life, anyway, though it hasn't been so long a one as mine; a vurry advent'rous life, I'd say. Might a man ask what's your callin', anyway?"

Harvey Crook laughed. "My trade," he said, "is— but I don't think it has any name of its own; unless you like to call me a carrier!"

"*A* carrier, Mr. Crook?"

"Well, yes, a carrier for profit, you might say. You see, I'm a man who's very much alone in the world, so far as relations go, and I've a great taste for moving about the earth in search of whatever may turn up. I don't need a great deal of money for that, but I need some, and, like other men, I like to have enough. My trade depends wholly on the fact that what may be cheap in one part of the world may be dear in another. So I buy in the cheapest market and sell in the dearest, according to the divine laws of Manchester. But I'm not always buying and selling, you understand, like a dealer—though perhaps that is what I am, after all. I am a specialist in things sufficiently profitable to make steady trading unnecessary—even impracticable. For instance, I have bought orchids in South America for shillings and sold them in London for hundreds of pounds. Though, of course, orchid-hunting is a pretty regular trade in the hands of some."

"Oh yes, I've heard of that caper; and a good trade, too. So you're a judge of orchids, eh?"

"Orchids and—other things. I was after orchids in South America when I got a rough diamond from an aborigine, a Botacudo—a very shy sort they are, and treacherous—for a good large hunting-knife. It wasn't a great diamond, you understand, but it was worth a few hundreds—pounds, you know, not dollars—and that was a good deal more than the knife cost—though it was a good one!

"I don't always bring things home to sell, of course; sometimes I take them out. I remember I once bought a very old Chinese manuscript roll in London for ten shillings, on speculation. I hadn't a ghost of a notion what it was all about, I admit—I haven't now—and it was pure luck; but the next time I was in China—I got there as soon as I could after the relief of the Legation at Pekin, of course—I found some old pundit who made no difficulty in bringing out a thousand trade dollars for it—about a hundred pounds on the exchange—so that I've a suspicion it was worth a good bit more. And this trip to India, too, I took something. I found some absurd clockwork figures in Switzerland that a watch-maker had made to amuse himself—little dolls that walked about on a platform and bowed and fanned themselves, and struck the hour with their fists on a bell. They were a bit out of order and tarnished, but a very small job put that right, and I got my price, and a very good one it was, from a Maharajah. An Indian prince with money to spend is like a child for toys."

"And are you bringing anything good back with you?"

"Well, very little of my own. There's something rather interesting belonging to another man, however; a dozen magnums of Tokay—the sweet imperial, I believe, the real stuff, and most amazingly old."

"Old?" queried Lyman W. Merrick, who had a proper respect for the antique. "What would you call old, now, in Imperial Tokay?"

"The exact vintage of this I don't know," Crook answered; "but the owner tells me it's eighty years in bottle, and that's something very special in any wine, I think."

"Eighty years! You don't say! And what might it have cost?"

"That I can't tell you either. I believe he came on it very cheap in a deal—he's a dealer in everything; a man named Hahn. But he expects to get a hundred pounds for the case, or pretty near it."

"That's very near eight and a half pounds a bottle, as I figure it. Forty-two dollars, any way; no bad price for a bottle of wine."

"They're magnums, of course."

"Yes, and Tokay isn't sloppin' around every day, even new, I guess. Come to think of it, I don't ever remember to have as much as seen a bottle of Tokay."

"Very few have; and fewer still have tasted it. More, nine-tenths of the few who have tasted it—or think they have—have only tried the adulterated stuff expanded by the wine merchants from the inferior brands of Tokay."

"Is that so?" commented Mr. Merrick absently.

Then he added, "Say, is that case of wine in the hold?"

"No—I've got it in my cabin.   I don't carry much with me, as a rule—a good deal less than most people take for a week's journey—and so there was no difficulty."

Mr. Merrick returned to the subject later. He had told his daughter of this case of the renowned and mysterious Imperial Tokay, and Daisy was all agog with the romance of the thing. Imperial Tokay was a thing she had read about, vaguely and mysteriously, but never seen—like bird's-nest soup, and haunted houses. She had read of the wonderful first quality of this rare Hungarian wine, and of how it was the produce of the grape-juice exuded by the mere pressure of the piled weight of the ripe fruit itself; of how even the lower qualities were bought by great favour among a narrow circle of Hungarian notables, and of how throughout Europe the name and little else was known; and she longed to peep inside the case, and at the very least, gaze upon the venerable bottles.

When Mr. Merrick referred to the Tokay again, he wanted to know how such a wine would be sold.

"They'd scarcely put it up in one lot, would they?" he asked.

"No—probably a bottle at a time, I should say, in the case of a great curiosity like this."

"Very well, Mr. Harvey Crook, here is business. Your friend expects, with luck, to make an average eight pounds and a half a bottle out of this wine, selling them separately. Now I'm mighty cur'ous about this wine, and I offer ten pounds for a bottle—fifty dollars, right here! And we'll try the liquor together; there!"

Harvey Crook shook his head. "Sorry," he said, "but I can't do it, possibly. The wine isn't mine, and I'm under engagement to take it to England safely, and then do with it what the owner tells me."

"But he's a dealer, and he only wants his money, I guess!"

"Very likely, but that's his business. Mine is to see it safely to England as it is."

"I'll give fifteen pounds—seventy-five dollars. There!"

Harvey Crook shook his head again, with a smile. "Very sorry," he said, "but I really can't! It isn't as though this stuff were mine, you see. It's given me in trust. No doubt Hahn would be ready enough to take the money, but he isn't here to do it. And of course I'd be glad to oblige you if I could—indeed I should much like to try the wine myself, as you so hospitably suggest—but I can't, you see!"

The days went on, and by dint of having nothing to do but think about the Tokay, Lyman W. Merrick began to desire it more urgently than ever.

"Come now, Mr. Harvey Crook," he exclaimed one long afternoon, "I'll speculate! I'll buy that case of wine, for one thousand dollars! One thousand dollars is two hundred pounds of English money—just twice what the owner expected. I'll buy the case and we'll try a bottle; and if our curiosity's satisfied with that, I'll put up the other eleven to auction as soon as ever we get ashore, and just see what comes of the little gamble. Is it a deal?"

This certainly seemed a more likely offer than the other. True, Crook had no authority to sell the wine, but he knew it was to be sold, and he had Hahn's word that he would be glad to take a hundred pounds for it. This was not an offer to break into the dozen, like the other, but one of double the dealer's price for the lot; yet Crook hesitated, in view of his instructions.

That evening Daisy Merrick took the matter up, and Daisy was an extremely persuasive young lady. Her father was so awfully set on tasting real old Imperial Tokay for once in his life that it would be real mean for anybody on earth to thwart him. Surely Mr. Crook didn't want to be thought real mean? And the dealer with his wife and family—why, he would be real mad if he found that Mr. Crook had refused an offer of actually double his price. Surely Mr. Crook didn't want the poor dealer to be real mad?

That decided Harvey Crook—that argument and Miss Daisy Merrick's persuasions; though it is only fair to say that the argument gathered a deal of weight from what Crook remembered of Hahn and his habits of business. Hahn would do anything for a shade of extra profit, and the man who stood in the way of a deal which would give Hahn double price for anything would be Hahn's enemy for life. On the other hand, he pictured Hahn's delight on receiving that double price without turning a hand himself to get it. He was in charge of Hahn's interests in the matter of that case of wine, and he would be neglecting them to refuse such an offer as this. So he took the responsibility and the two hundred pounds, and the case of magnums of Imperial Tokay, eighty years at least in bottle and an indefinite number in wood beforehand, became the property of Lyman W. Merrick, of Merricksville, Pennsylvania.

The case was taken into his cabin and the boards lifted from the top. Hahn had gone to a vast deal of trouble in packing, and there was a deal of sawdust and chips to be shifted before the muddy old seal of one of the big bottles showed itself. The bottle was carefully withdrawn, and the packing replaced, with another bottle, empty, to fill out the space.

After dinner next day the bottle of Tokay was produced in full state. With great care the seal was removed and the soddened old cork withdrawn. The wine was of a fine rich green colour, sweet and curious; but to both Merrick and Crook it seemed to have suffered from over-age; though because of the unfamiliarity of the wine it was not easy to be certain.

Mr. Merrick was hospitable with his precious wine, and two or three other passengers tried it and made their comments; and then the rest of the big bottle was carefully decanted.

"Now if I was like some parties I've met," said Merrick, "I'd ha' gone advertising myself with that wine, and playin' the coruscatin' millionaire, dealin' out all there is to the passengers, whether they wanted my blamed wine or not, and getting it in the papers when I go ashore. But that's not quite my style. Here's enough for a glass after dinner when I want it, or any friend of mine—though I must say, after all, I'd as well take a Chartreuse, or rather—and the rest goes into the sale-rooms, and then we'll just see how I come out for the bottle."

So the voyage went, and as Southampton was neared, Mr. Merrick's interest began to be transferred from the case of Tokay to the tour before him.

"I want to see England," he said once to Crook, "for reasons. I've been there once before, by myself, but I had to do it all in a hurry, and some of the time went in trying to find an old friend of mine—a real good friend he was, though I've seen mighty little of him altogether. He did me the best turn of my life, sir—yes; and I'm going to try once again now, though I'm afraid I'm a bit late. But try I will, and it's for that reason that I want to see England more than I

wanted to see India. Though Daisy has some pretty
wide plans of her own, too."

This, indeed, was the truth, and between them father
and daughter had "fixed up" a most amazing programme by the time they were within a few hours'
steam of Southampton; a programme in which the British
Isles, show places, scenery and everything, were to be
got over at the rate of about two thousand square miles
a-day. A programme, indeed, that would have grown
more crowded still were it not that an accident interrupted the process of programme-fixing; for after a
whole voyage of perfectly exemplary behaviour on the
part of the engines, the propeller-shaft went wrong in
course of the last few hours, and the *Rajapur* at last
made an ignominious entry into Southampton Water at
the tail end of a tow-rope, with a fussy, smoky little
tug to pull it. The accident distracted attention from
the programme, and made the landing in Southampton
half a day late or more; so that it also had the effect,
between the lateness of the landing and the immensity
of the scheme of tour, of causing the auction-sale of the
magnums of Tokay to be squeezed into the first few
hours ashore at Southampton.

And there, in fact, it took place, as soon as the wine could be got through the Customs, with a disastrous end to Lyman W. Merrick's little gamble. For the bottles, duly divided into eleven lots, were "starred" into the catalogue of the handiest local sale, and would there have gone for a shilling or two apiece, were it not that some of the *Rajapur* passengers, who had heard of the speculation, turned up and bid for a bottle here and there; and a wine-merchant's traveller of some enterprise took four lots at ten shillings a lot.

So that Mr. Merrick got back nearly five pounds of his two hundred, which, he said, would pay the duty, anyway, and leave him with the eternal glory of having consumed a bottle of wine costing nine hundred and seventy-five dollars, and such consolation as the glory might bring him.

The report of this uncommercial ending to Merrick's speculation in Imperial Tokay reached Harvey Crook by letter—a letter written, as soon as the sale had closed, by Daisy Merrick. It had been arranged that this should be done when Crook bade his friends goodbye before the sale. He would have stayed to see it, but the delay in the *Rajapur's* arrival made it impossible; for by a letter sent across from Brindisi he had made a certain appointment in London which he could now barely keep.

It was a short and simple enough letter that Crook received from Daisy Merrick,—a few sentences and no more, conveying the result of the sale, and a short message from Daisy's father as to the possibility of meeting Crook again in England. A trivial short letter, with nothing in it to call for careful preservation—nothing at all. And yet Crook refolded it very carefully, returned it to its envelope, and packed it away in the safest compartment of his pocket-book. It was not easy to guess why, perhaps; for Crook was not ordinarily an over-careful man with his correspondence.

IV.

THE next day, at Standish's Hotel in London, Harvey Crook had barely finished his lunch, when he was brought a card—a card which filled him with amazement. For it was the card of Mr. Frank Hahn!

"Show him up," said Crook, in blank wonder.

Hahn it was, sure enough.

"Ha! my dear Crook," he exclaimed effusively, offering his hand, "how are you? You're surprised to see me, of course. But the fact is, I pulled round so quickly that I was able to catch the mail-boat, and I came overland with the mails from Brindisi; so I've been in London some days, you see. I've been here to-day once before, but you were out, and I went to the docks before that—didn't know whether you'd get out at Southampton or come right on, you see. I'm eternally obliged to you, my dear chap, about the Tokay, you know, though as it turns out I needn't have bothered you after all. I'll clear it out of your way. Where is it?"

"I haven't got it; it's sold."

"Sold?" Such a look of blank horror fell across Hahn's face that Harvey Crook started where he stood. "Sold? What d'ye mean?"

"I had a big offer for it on the voyage—double your best price—so of course I closed for you. Two hundred pounds."

"*What!* Two hundred pounds? Heavens, you—you—you—I—I'm ruined!"

3 *

Hahn sank into a chair, white and gasping.

"Ruined?" retorted Crook. "Skittles! You put the outside price at a hundred yourself!"

Hahn sat staring and distraught.

"I—I won't have it!" he said. "You—you're responsible! I—I demand my property—you're responsible, I tell you!"

"Yes, I suppose I am," Crook replied, getting angry. "Very well, here's the money—the very notes I took for it; and now my responsibility is at an end. Two hundred. I took the stuff for you as a favour, when the most you hoped to get out of it was a hundred—for your wife and children, you remember; and I get you two hundred for it, and you howl about my responsibility!"

"It's a robbery," cried Hahn wildly. "A robbery! I want it back! You shan't do me like that!"

"Get out before I do you with my boot!" Crook retorted angrily. "Get out!"

"No, Crook—no, of course I didn't mean that. It ain't for me to call it a robbery, perhaps you think, but it was sharp practice, wasn't it now, Crook? It *was* sharp practice, and you're a deal cuter than I took you for, Crook. But come now, we can arrange this. I'll take you into it, and we'll see about it together. Do the fair thing with a pal, Crook. Where is it?"

"Where is it? All over the place by now. I sold it to an American on the boat, and we drank a bottle. Then he put the rest up to auction at Southampton, and it ought to be a consolation to you to know that it fetched about a fiver, all the eleven bottles. Take your money and clear out—I'm a bit tired of you."

"Who sold it?" Hahn asked eagerly, gathering his faculties again. "Who was the auctioneer?"

"A man named Lawson — up by the Memorial Hall."

Hahn started up, seized the notes and took his hat. Then he paused and said, with a curiously intent expression, "You and the American tried a bottle. How did you find it? Anything unusual, eh?"

"Old Tokay's always unusual, isn't it?" Crook answered. "It's a green wine, and very sweet."

"And you emptied it, quite to the bottom?" Still Hahn regarded Crook with the same intent gaze.

"Yes—we decanted it."

Hahn's steady look persisted for a few seconds and then he turned and hurried out.

.   .   .   .   .

Harvey Crook sat mightily astonished for about ten minutes.   Then he began to think the thing out. "Ruined—plenty for both—take me into it—anything unusual—what was he driving at?" he mused.

Certain things were quite plain.   This wine, the value of which Hahn had put at a hundred pounds, was clearly, for some mysterious reason or other, worth a very great deal more—to Hahn.   Also, it was pretty obvious that Hahn's "touch of fever" at Delhi had been all a sham.   Its object was not very difficult to divine.   For some reason or another Hahn had wished to have that case of Tokay brought home by another person—wished it to be in some other person's possession even during the later part of his stay in India —and yet to be in perfectly safe keeping.   Why, seeing that he regarded it as so valuable a possession? There could only be one reason for that—fear of the consequences if it were found in *his* possession.   But why, again?   He had bought or traded for the wine openly, it was plain, or he would not have talked of it so readily and unreservedly. From these considerations and from Hahn's unguarded expressions it became clear to Harvey Crook that there must have been something in that case more valuable than wine, however rare and costly.

And with that a thought struck him like a bullet. The Eye of Goona!

Hahn was notoriously quite a well-to-do man; that talk of the importance of a hundred pounds to his wife and family was pure gammon, as was very plain from his indifference to the two hundred the wine had fetched. The wife and family themselves were also gammon, probably. But the Eye of Goona—that would be a prize for the richest man alive.

The notion seemed a trifle extravagant at first, but as he thought it out every consideration confirmed his suspicions. What else should Hahn be afraid to have in his belongings, in Delhi? It would be a portable sort of thing, easily carried about in a waistcoat pocket, anywhere. But the hue and cry was up, and anybody might have been searched. More, the ways of Indian princes and their retainers were apt to be subtle and unconventional. If a thief could be

got to creep undetected into a Rajah's guarded tent,
another, who might also be an assassin, could be com-
missioned to get into a European dealer's quarters with
the like secrecy.

Then the obvious practicability of the thing was
to be considered. Assuming, to begin with, that the
stolen green diamond had found its way into Hahn's
possession, what course of action could possibly be
more natural than the one he had adopted? To carry it
about with him among invisible emissaries of the Rajah
who might have unsuspected clues to its whereabouts
would have been to risk its loss—very probably to risk
death. To hide it would be the obvious expedient—
to hide it in some movable object which might go out
of the country unsuspected. What more likely place of
concealment than in a dark bottle of old wine? And
here a significant fact presented itself. The Eye of
Goona was of oval shape, and just a trifle more than
an inch wide. That would never have passed the neck
of an ordinary wine bottle—but these were magnums.
The neck of a magnum would be large enough just to
let such a jewel slip comfortably through. Then the
cork might be replaced, the old seal carefully counter-

feited, and all made snug in that innocent case of a dozen magnums.

Plainly something of the sort had ,been done, and plainly the concealed object must be a jewel of some sort. What else of so great value could be kept in such a bottle? For if any one thing was certain in this astonishing business, it was that it was *in a bottle,* and not loose in the case, that the valuable object was concealed. Hahn's pointed inquiries as to the bottle that had been opened were sufficient assurance of that. And he had gone off in a hurry to find the auctioneer, and no doubt so trace the dispersed bottles.

So much being assumed, and so much proved, Hahn's trick in putting on him the danger and responsibility of getting the plunder home was easy enough to understand. Hahn had shammed fever, but waited till he was safely off in the *Rajapur,* and then had hastened to get ahead of him by mail-boat and overland route, to receive the prize safely in London. More, his passage must have been booked long before in the mail-boat, for it was because of the early engagement of all the berths that the Merricks, and Crook himself, had come in the slower *Rajapur*.

As to the plunder everything pointed to the Eye. What other great jewel had been lost? And at any rate, Eye of Goona or not, the gem must be one of extraordinary value, from all the evidence. The exact circumstances of the robbery must still remain in some doubt; there was, at present, no telling how the jewel had reached Hahn's hands, nor what was the explanation of the dummy stone found in the hands of the slain thief. But putting these doubts aside for the moment, the bare fact seemed to emerge very clearly in Harvey Crook's mind; there was a jewel of fabulous value in one of those eleven bottles of wine, now dispersed by sale. Hahn had tricked him—had put upon him the whole risk of transporting his plunder into safe quarters, and was now in agonised pursuit of that same plunder by way of the auctioneer. Harvey Crook resolved to join in the chase himself, and get ahead of Hahn if he could.

"My trade," he thought to himself; "plainly it is in my trade. That rascal has stolen the stone, and if I can get hold of it, it should cost me very little here in England. But carried to India, it should bring a pretty handsome sum from the Rajah of Goona. I don't want the jewel, for it isn't mine. But neither is it Hahn's; and since I brought it here to please him, I see no reason why I shouldn't take it back to please myself—and the Rajah. Come—there should be fun in it, as well as money!"

II.

MR. NORIE'S MAGNUM.

I.

HARVEY CROOK pulled out his watch with one hand, and with the other he pressed the electric bell. In two minutes he was comparing his watch with the tables of a railway guide. There would be a train from Waterloo for Southampton at three precisely, and with any reasonable luck that train would enable him to reach the auctioneer's office before it closed at six. Twenty-five minutes was all he had to catch this train, and he realised that he must hurry. He sent the waiter for a hansom and selected a kit-bag from his luggage. In this bag he commonly kept all he needed for his immediate wants, and now a glance showed him that it was sufficient. He took out a carefully tied roll rather less than two feet long, and glanced about him as if doubtful where to leave it. Finally he put it back in the bag. It was almost the only rarity—the only piece of stock—he happened to have with him, and it had originally come from China. For the moment he could not think of a suitable place in which to stow it, so, since it was a light matter enough, he resolved to carry it with him. Indeed, since, in a search after the Tokay, he would probably have to deal with persons interested in rarities, this particular article might serve as a convenient introduction, and, in any extreme event, possibly as an object of trade or barter.

The waiter made a lucky choice with the hansom, and all fear of losing the train vanished in the first five minutes of the trot; though it was plain that every cab-rider at that moment was not so fortunate, for in Cranborne Street Crook passed another hansom which had come to grief. The cabman was unbuckling the traces from his fallen horse, while his unfortunate fare was desperately collecting a number of articles which had scattered from a burst portmanteau—a portmanteau that had evidently fallen endwise from the roof. The man looked up as Crook's cab passed, and Crook was interested—probably a little gratified—to perceive that it was Hahn himself who was thus being delayed at the beginning of the race.

Waterloo was gained with a margin of four minutes, and all was so far satisfactory—for Crook. Not so for Hahn, however, for as the train left the platform Crook saw him once again, running his hardest, with his broken portmanteau tied round with string, while a galloping porter ran at his heels to prevent him risking his life. The porter, having nothing to carry, ran the faster, and, seized Hahn by the arms from behind; and Crook's last view of him comprised a heap, whereof the broken portmanteau formed the base, and the zealous porter the apex, with the baffled Hahn sprawling between them.

Having thus scored the first trick, Harvey Crook sat back well content. Two other men were in the carriage, both younger than himself, in animated conversation. For some while Crook paid no attention to this, but turned over the evening paper he had brought with him. Presently, however, he threw this aside, and then he could no longer avoid hearing.

He had set the young men down as artists from the beginning, and now it grew plain that he had been right. One was a sculptor and the other a painter, and much of their talk had reference to another painter, familiarly referred to as "Charley." Charley, it would seem, was something of a practical wag—a character which Crook had himself met among painters more than once.

"I'm a score behind with Charley," said the sculptor, "and I must make it even somehow. Did you hear about the awful row at my little show?"

"Something about a drunken model, wasn't it? Tell me."

"Drunken model? I believe you. But it was Charley that worked the thing. Ha! ha! But it really wasn't so bad, while it lasted, though it gave awful jumps to some of my respected patrons. You should have been there."

"Always keep out of show days—except my own. Can't help being *there,* you know."

"No—I sympathise; the sort of people that go round on show Sundays and such—well there, that's enough—never mind 'em now. I was showing that thing of mine for the new park, open space, or whatever it is—you know, the alderman in his robes; that

and the bust of the Mayor of Dumbledore. Well, all
the friends of the alderman and the Mayor turned up,
as I expected they would, and they brought their
sisters and their cousins, though I should judge that the
larger part of the female visitors were aunts—fat ones.
I did all I could to make things comfortable—not to
say splendid. Hired a carpet and two dozen chairs,
and got in the necessary tuck from the pastrycook's.
And I thought I'd have Boaler to wait, in an eighteenth
century dress and wig. Know Boaler?"

"Know of him; never employed him. Big model,
for muscles and all that, isn't he?"

"That's the fellow—an uncommon fine old chap for
anything of that sort, though he is getting a trifle old
and he drinks a lot. He's been posing to me for the
Prehistoric Man I'm on for the next Academy, and
mighty well he does it, with a bearskin hearthrug tied
round him and a cow's jawbone in his hand. Well,
you know, I thought he'd look rather fine in silk stock-
ings and velvet breeches, with a gold-laced coat and a
powdered wig, announcing people from the door and
handing round a tray afterwards. And so he would—
if he'd done it; but the old wretch didn't." Here the

young sculptor flung himself back against the cushions with a burst of laughter.

"I got a capital suit for him," he went on presently, "fitted excellently—borrowed it from Haslam. I impressed on him that he must be up to time—dressed and ready by half-past three. He promised he would, but he didn't." The sculptor laughed again.

"He didn't," he repeated. "I had to go out, and didn't get back till nearly four. There was the gold-laced suit hanging up in the little room at the back, but Boaler wasn't in it—wasn't there at all, in fact. The result was I had to meet the people at the door myself, and skip the announcing. They came crowding in, and—well you know the sort of thing that happens on these occasions; women in fine dresses all doing the haughty and superfine, and the man the place belongs to doing the humble and complaisant. I kept looking and longing for the nefarious Boaler, but he didn't come, and I had to go dancing about with tea and macaroons, and try to do the whole thing myself. In the middle of the agony Charley came in.

"'It's all right,' he whispered, "Boaler's here—I met him. He's gone in the back way and he's getting into his uniform. I'll go and hurry him up.' And off he went; and he *did* hurry him up!

"He *did* hurry him up. Lord! He did! The people had left off walking about, and all the two dozen chairs were full of supercilious old aldermanesses and mayoresses with tea-cups, when the inner door opened, and, with a shove from behind, in staggered the infamous Boaler, full as a barrel, in the uniform of prehistoric man, bearskin rug and cow's jawbone complete! And worse—while he waved the jawbone in one hand he carried a pewter pot in the other, and a clay pipe in his mouth, and he smiled and smiled and swayed and swayed till he came down in a heap! Heavens! The row! The mayoresses and the aldermanesses and the haughty and the superfine! It beat everything!"

"Broke up the show, of course."

"Broke it up? Broke up's too mild a term. I never saw anything like it; the place might have been on fire! They're the sort of people that never see the humour of anything, and because I laughed—who wouldn't?—I believe they thought I'd done the whole thing on purpose!"

"And it was Charley, was it?"

"Chiefly, though certainly Boaler himself gave him the idea. You see, the old ruffian had given way to his usual failing, and when he began to change, by force of habit he got into the prehistoric rig instead of the proper dress. Charley, going in to hurry him up, found him like that and rather liked the idea, so he added the pipe and pot by way of final touches and shoved him into the studio. Says he intended it as a lesson for Boaler, against the sin of intemperance! Tells me I ought to be nearly as grateful as Boaler himself, because it was such a fine preliminary advertisement for the Prehistoric Man at the Academy!"

The two young men laughed loud and long, and lit their pipes; and then their talk drifted off into more immediately professional matters. And so two hours more went, and at last the train pulled up at Southampton.

4*

II.

It was a little late—more than a quarter of an hour late, in fact—and Crook had only a few minutes in which to reach the office of Lawson the auctioneer. He got a fly, but it crawled as that sort of fly does, and the clocks had finished striking six ere the office drew in sight. Lawson's clerk, in fact, was in the act of locking the front door, and when he turned away he met Harvey Crook as he jumped from the fly.

"Good evening," said Crook; "I'm afraid I'm a bit late. I want to ask about a few lots you sold last Thursday."

The clerk looked uncomfortably up the street.

"I've shut the office," he said. "Can't you come in the morning?"

"Of course it's past office hours," Crook replied; "but I suppose you're open to do work on your own account after office hours? Suppose we say at a guinea an hour?"

The clerk opened his eyes wide.

"Well, yes," he said, "I should think so; at a guinea an hour." But there was a deal of doubt in his voice.

"That's what I mean," answered Crook, "and here's a guinea in advance for the first hour, though I shan't keep you so long."

And he handed over a sovereign and a shilling.

"Well," the clerk answered, still rather distrustfully, "what is it you want me to do? Nothing against the office interests, mind!"

"Of course not—nothing at all. Mr. Lawson would do it himself if he were here, but he isn't. In Thursday's sale there were eleven magnums of Tokay wine, put in by a travelling American gentleman named Merrick. I want to know who bought them."

"Let's see," said the clerk thoughtfully. "They were 'starred' into the catalogue, weren't they?"

"Yes—Mr. Merrick only brought them in on the morning of the sale."

"Well, I can tell you one buyer from memory. That was Mr. Norie, the artist. He had one bottle."

"Do you know him?"

"Oh, yes—everybody about here knows him; his father belonged to Southampton."

"And the others?"

"That won't be so easy. You see, they were mostly bids for money down from strangers, and the buyers took them straight away. But come into the office."

The clerk pulled out his key again, and unlocked the door. He was a quick young man with dark little eyes, and a smiling, though not handsome, face. He carefully shut the door behind him, pushed up the lid of a desk, and brought out an interleaved and marked catalogue.

"Mind you," he said, "I'm not doing any more than we'd do for almost anybody who came and asked—in office hours. I'm not doing anything that Lawson would disapprove of, and I won't. Here you are. Lot 87 star, one magnum real old Imperial Tokay, reputed eighty years in bottle. Lot 88 star, ditto; lot 89 star, ditto; and so on to lot 97 star, ditto, the last of 'em. There's prices and all: 87 star, money paid down, no name; 88 star, Smith—might as well be no name at all; 89 star, Smith also—and Smith's the name to the next two."

These lots, in fact, had all been bought by the same Smith—the wine merchant's traveller. But Crook knew nothing of this, and the clerk went on.

"Ninety-two star is Allen, eight shillings."

Allen was a passenger on the *Rajapur,* Crook remembered, though again he said nothing. This would give him another advantage over Hahn.

"Ninety-three star, no name, money paid. By the way, you know," the clerk pursued, "all the money was paid down for these lots, as I can tell by the ticks, but some people gave their names and some didn't. Ninety-four star—that was Mr. Norie's. He took it away with him under his arm."

"An artist, you say?"

"Yes; but if you're thinking of buying of him—was that what you wanted?"

"Well, yes; that was it."

"Well, I don't suppose he'll sell. He isn't poor although he's an artist, and he buys things for his own fancy. He bought an old pair of candlesticks at the same sale, and took them away, too, in his pockets."

"Very well. He lives here, of course?"

"Yes—I'll show you the way, if you like. He has rooms in London, too, but his studio's here. Ninety-five star is Curtice, ten shillings; and the last two have no names."

"Very well—that'll do. And now, where is Mr. Norie's studio?"

The clerk shut his desk and came into the street again, carefully locking the door behind him.

"Keep along past the bend in the road," he said, "till the road forks, and then keep to the right. The road will lead you out of the town past some new villas with a row of old trees—elms—in front of them. In the middle of the villas there is a short turning—a lane —and the only house in that turning is Mr. Norie's studio, just behind the villas."

"Thank you," said Harvey Crook, as he turned to go. "And now perhaps you'll give me your private address. If I have anything else for you—on the same terms—I suppose you won't mind my calling and saying so, eh?"

"Not a bit. My name's Symons, and 14 Waterview Terrace is my address. Is that all?"

"I think so, at present. Will you be at home all the evening?"

"At home? Oh yes, I shall be at home if you want me. Good night."

Crook returned to his fly and drove to the Royal Hotel for dinner. This he took at once, and then made the best of his way to Mr. Norie's studio.

It was now full night, but not very dark. The next train from London had been in some little time, and it was reasonable to suppose that Hahn was now in Southampton. What would he do? The auctioneer's office was shut; probably he would have to be content with his dinner for that evening's work.

Harvey Crook walked smartly in the direction of the villas with the row of elms before them, and was not long in getting clear of the town. He passed a market-garden or two and a small meadow, and so reached the elms and the villas they shadowed. There was no possibility of mistake in the matter of Mr. Norie's studio. There it stood, as the auctioneer's clerk had said, alone in the little lane that divided the villas into two rows.

It looked as though it might be a good studio.

There was a long sloping roof on the north side, with a row of skylights, and roomy-looking blocks on the opposite side that seemed to be comfortable living and sleeping rooms. There was nothing but a door in the front wall of the studio, and that wall extended left and right to make a boundary for a little garden. Harvey Crook knocked at the door.

There was no answer. He repeated the knock, louder, and after a minute or two more discovered a bell, and knocked and rang furiously. It grew plain that Mr. Norie was out.

Now it would never do to go back without another attempt. There was a chance—ten to one against, certainly; but that is no bad chance as things go—that the Eye of Goona itself lay in that modest little brick building. Hahn was in Southampton, and by aid of judicious inquiry he might learn of the situation of this particular magnum of Tokay at any minute. He might even contrive to get hold of Norie himself in some club or billiard-room in the town. Harvey Crook resolved to watch the building all night, if necessary.

Beyond the villas the road rose on a hill, which overlooked the studio and the town beyond. Crook went on up the hill, turning an occasional glance back toward the studio as he went. Dim in the moonlight lay the outlines of the town and the water beyond, and lights twinkled in thick clusters. Turning to look at the studio once again after some minutes of walking, he clearly descried some dark object moving before the white frame of the skylight. What was this? Burglary? Could it be possible that Hahn was taking this short cut to the bottle of Tokay? Crook hurried down the hill at top speed.

He turned the corner by the villas, and approached the studio by springing strides on tiptoe. Plainly enough in the half-light he could see not one, but two men, mounting the skylight, the hindmost man with his leg hanging over the boundary wall. This was lucky. What better introduction to the owner than to seize burglars as they were entering the place? Busy at their work, the men had not perceived him. He ran up and seized the dangling leg with both hands.

There was a hasty exclamation from above, and the owner of the leg made a quick grab at the skylight frame to save himself from falling. "Who's that?" he cried indignantly, peering back over his shoulder. "What are you after?"

"Well, if it comes to that," replied Crook, holding on his tightest, "who are *you,* and what are *you* after?" Though, indeed, he rather fancied he recognised the voice.

The man on the wall changed hands, turned round and peered down closer. "Why, hullo!" he said. "Don't I know you somewhere?"

And Crook thought it very likely, for he recognised one of the young men who had travelled with him in the train.

"Have you come to see Charlie Norie?" continued the young man on the wall; "because he's out."

"Yes, I have. But you don't expect I'm going away leaving two men breaking into his house, do you? Just because one of the burglars tells me he's out?"

The young man burst into a grin. "I say, Jack," he called to his companion, who seemed to be half-way in the skylight, "he thinks we're burglars!"

There was a stifled laugh from the direction of the

skylight, and another head came poking over the shoulder of the man whose leg Crook was grasping.

"It's all right," said the head; "it's only a bit of a plant on Charley." And by the voice Crook knew that the head belonged to the young sculptor of Prehistoric Man.

"Look here," the sculptor went on, after a moment's pause, "you come in yourself, if you want to see it's all right. We're both friends of Charley's—just as much as you are. We're only chalking up a score on him!"

The thing was plain enough now. This Norie, who had bought the magnum of Tokay, was the Charley of the railway-carriage conversation, and the raid now in progress was by way of reprisal for the Boaler outrage. An idea struck Harvey Crook.

"All right," he said, "I'll come. You drop in through the skylight, or we'll be attracting attention." And with that he released the other's leg.

The sculptor dropped through the skylight and struck a match within, and his companion, after giving Crook a hand up, speedily followed.

"What were you thinking of doing?" asked Crook, when they were all three safe on the studio floor.

"Well, we didn't quite know," replied Jack, the sculptor, looking about him after striking a light. "We rather trusted to what we might find, not having been down here for some time. By the way—I say, you know, you're the man that came down in the same carriage!"

"Quite right—I know! And I didn't let on. But I wasn't to know you meant the same Charley, was I? But don't waste time, or he'll be back. There's one sell I can put you up to. He's just bought a magnum of old Imperial Tokay."

"Imperial Tokay? Exorbitant sybarite! Come, that certainly ought *not* to be allowed. A whole magnum of real Tokay for Charley Norie, while far more deserving persons like ourselves have never even smelt the divine tipple! As free-born Britons we must see into this. Come, I know where he keeps his liquor, anyhow!"

The studio was handsomely furnished, though somewhat sparsely. Jack made straight for a fine old Dutch standing cupboard close by the door, wide and high, with a pair of large painted doors. He swung the doors open and disclosed many shelves of many bottles, intermingled with glasses and soda-syphons. Conspicuous among them all, lying on its side because of its height, was the magnum of Tokay. Crook picked it up and passed it to the others.

"There it is," he said simply.

Jack Knowles regarded it thoughtfully. "Problem is," he said, "to open it without ruining the seal. Not that the seal isn't pretty well ruined already." And, indeed, the old yellow seal was cracked and rubbed out of all distinctive shape.

"Not difficult," observed Crook, taking the bottle back. "I'll try. We can make it all right with a lighted match if you want to shut it up afterward. Do you?"

"I think," remarked Jack Knowles, sagely, "that the obvious course dictated by justice and humanity is that we remove from our dear friend's reach—from this bottle, in fact—the temptation to excessive drinking which has proved so fatal in the case of the unhappy Boaler. I will undertake to find two or three empty bottles in which the removal may be accomplished—he always keeps 'em on the bottom shelf. This being effected, in order to prevent the shock our dear friend might experience on discovering his great bottle absolutely empty, we will proceed to fill it up with a judicious admixture of more wholesome but less expensive liquors selected from the other bottles in this cupboard. Vinegar, for instance, and rum, with a little sauterne to give it paleness, and a modicum of mustard to impart body. Then, when our friend has been disgusted with his luxurious indulgence by taking a sample, we will restore him to a proper frame of mind by inviting him to *our* rooms, to try *our* real old Imperial Tokay! I think that's the proper—not to say the moral—course?"

His friend assented heartily, and Crook proceeded to remove the cork with great care to avoid breaking it up. He had already, with a sharp, broad blade of his pocket-knife, cut away the top of the seal in a single slice, and carefully laid it aside. With a little humouring the old cork came away whole, though with a bad crack across it; and now Crook stood with the opened bottle in his hand, and a rather ticklish task before him. Whether or not that bottle contained the Green

Eye of Goona would be decided in a few minutes—seconds, rather; and it was his task to ascertain the fact without the knowledge of the two rattle-brained humorists before him, both with their eyes intently fixed on that big bottle, with never a suspicion in the world of what an enormous matter it might carry in its depths.

"Steady!" he said; "this wine has been in bottle eighty years, as I happen to know. It would be a pity to run the risk of spoiling it in the decanting. You are much too mercurial for the job. My hand is particularly steady—you rout out the empty bottles and bring them."

In a moment a bottle was thrust into his hand. He turned evenly towards the light and slowly elevated the bottle between his eye and the gas-jet. Holding it by the neck, he very slowly and steadily tilted the magnum till its lip clinked on the lip of the smaller bottle, and the precious liquid began to trickle from one to the other. In this position, if the great green stone came rolling toward the mouth of the magnum he would probably be able to see it through the

The Green Eye of Goona. 5

dark glass of the neck, where both glass and wine were thinner.

Slowly and steadily the green wine rose in the small bottle till it reached the neck. Crook ceased pouring, and held it out. "Another bottle!" he demanded, keeping the magnum still tilted in the air. "Cork that one carefully—don't shake it!"

A second bottle was thrust into his left hand, and again he began to pour, slowly and warily. Nothing chinked in the magnum, nothing came sliding into the tapering neck to check the free flow of the wine. Probably it would not till the magnum was nearly emptied. So the second bottle was filled.

"Another!" cried Crook. "This will about empty it, I think. There should be a trifle under half a gallon."

And still he kept his eye fixed on the dim light that came through the neck of the magnum.

The wine rose gradually in the third bottle, and when it was about half full Crook cast his eye back along the magnum. At this angle, he judged, the jewel must come rolling forward now, if it were there at all. Still, he would rather it kept back till the bottle could be emptied. Higher and higher it went, and higher the wine rose in the small bottle, till at last the dregs ran out, and the third bottle was full. The thing was settled; the Eye of Goona was not there.

"Here you are," remarked Crook calmly; "that's the lot. Mark that third bottle—you must let it stand longer than the others. I'm afraid I poured a trifle too far, and there's sediment in it. Now select your varied poisons."

The young men turned to the cupboard, and Crook took the occasion to make assurance doubly sure. He up-ended the empty magnum on his palm and shook it, then lifted it to the light again and shook it once more. There was no doubt of it; no diamond was there.

"Come," cried Jack Knowles impatiently, "we've wasted too much time already—we mustn't bother too much about what goes into the empty bottle; that would be pampering Charley, and running risks our-selves. This is vinegar, anyhow, by the label, and here is a spoonful of mustard and some rum. There are plenty of other liquids here, and we'll leave the rest to luck—Charley's luck is always wonderful. In it all

5 *

goes. Thoughtful of him to provide a funnel, wasn't it?"

In it all went, indeed, and the old cork was forced down over the horrible mixture. After which the seal was carefully replaced and melted down at the cut edges with a match.

"And now," said Jack Knowles, when the magnum had been replaced where it had been found, "we will away. We did think of standing his lay figure against the police station and getting it locked up as drunk and incapable, but we mustn't disturb anything now—that would arouse unworthy suspicions. We will away, and do our awaying without a moment's delay. Up through the skylight, Sewell! Quick, before I turn out the light."

They left the studio as they had entered it, one at a time through the window, and Jack Knowles, coming last, handed out the three bottles with loving care. Then the skylight was shut down, and they all stood in the open lane.

"Beautiful arrangement, those skylights," commented Jack Knowles. "Perfect dispensation of Providence for a burglar. Easy to get at, and nothing to hold 'em down but the brass arm, which Charley never fastens. Some day he will positively be robbed!"

Crook, having ascertained the direction in which the others were going, instantly discovered that he must go the opposite way. And so he waited in the dark a little way beyond the elms, while the two young fellows went off laughing toward the town.

"Lucky they never thought of asking my name," he thought to himself. "Well, here's an end to the prospects of *that* magnum, at any rate, so far as I'm concerned. But there's no reason why it shouldn't occupy Hahn's attention for a bit longer—it would give me a start for the next. I think I'll see that auctioneer's clerk again before I go to bed."

So that as soon as the two friends were quite out of sight and hearing he set off for Waterview Terrace. He found it to be a row of neat little houses with gardens in front, and he was saved any trouble in making a quest for No. 14 by observing Symons, in his shirt-sleeves, with a lantern, industriously hunting for snails in his garden.

"Oh, you, is it, sir?" said Symons when he had ascertained his visitor's identity. "I'm on a snail hunt; I never knew 'em out so early as they are this year, and the only way to keep 'em down is to go for 'em after dark.   What is it now?"

"I'm going to take up a little more of your out-of-office time, if you don't mind, on the usual terms.   It's private."

"All right—I'll come and take a turn along the terrace, if you don't mind the shirt-sleeves."   And Mr. Symons put down his lantern and came out of his little green gate.

"About those magnums of Tokay, now," said Crook, as they walked along before the little gardens. "I want to buy them all; and I want to enlist your help.   Never mind about Mr. Norie's—I've been there.   But if you can get hold of any of the others I'll pay you five pounds a bottle for them, cash on the nail."

"Whew! you must be very fond of that wine?"

"Well—yes; as a collector, you see. I want to collect that lot.   But there's another collector in the field, and it's that I came to speak about. I expect he'll be round to the office first thing in the morning."

"Um!" said Symons. "Of course I can't break office rules."

"No—I don't want you to do it. You can tell him what the office records show—which is precious little. More, you can tell him about Mr. Norie, and give him his address—I want you to do it, in fact; he can't get the bottle, and it will delay him. Understand?"

"I think I do. I'll tell him all about Mr. Norie; but I'll give him as little about the other things as I can manage; always with due regard to office rules, of course."

"Of course. I see you understand. And to make things plainer, I'll tell you this. Not only will I give you five pounds for any bottle of that lot you may bring me, but I'll pay you five for every one I can get myself, with your aid. That's satisfactory, I hope?"

Mr. Symons' quick little eyes positively sparkled amid the darkness. "Satisfactory?" he said. "Rather! Handsome—handsome, I'm sure."

"Very well then, I hope I shall see you again soon. Meantime, to carry out the principle of cash in advance, here's a fiver for the first magnum, and I chance whether we get it or not!"

III.

MR. CHARLES NORIE, painter of marine subjects, was a tall young man of wide shoulders and a rather handsome, but more good-humoured, face. He was not dependent on his work for his livelihood, for his father, who had been a shipbuilder at Southampton, had left him quite a decent competence. His friends, Jack Knowles the sculptor and Harry Sewell the painter, had also connections in or about Southampton, and had come down for a week or two's holiday. Norie was in the habit of walking down into the town to take his dinner at an hotel, and his friends had taken advantage of this habit to raid his studio in his absence. But on the night following they all three dined together at the Dolphin, with another friend, one Kirk, a young surgeon of the neighbourhood.

"No," interposed Norie, when dinner was finished, "don't have liqueurs—I've got a treat for you at the studio. I picked up a magnum of real old Imperial Tokay the other day, at a sale down here. Never saw a bottle before in my life. We'll light up cigars and stroll along to the studio and open it. They tell me it's eighty years old, and you mustn't go spoiling your mouths with liqueurs first."

Jack Knowles and Harry Sewell chuckled inwardly, and avoided each other's eyes for fear of open laughter.

"That's a rarity," observed Kirk. "How did it come here?"

"Some fellow brought it ashore from a P. & O. boat, I believe, and put it in a sale at Lawson's. I shouldn't have known of it, but I went in after a pair of Sheffield candlesticks — I'll show 'em to you presently, they're capital. There were eleven magnums of Tokay, and I wish I'd bought more now, for it seems they were dirt cheap. I've had a fellow after mine today, offering a tenner for it, and almost begging me to take his money; and it only cost me half-a-sovereign!"

"I'd have taken it," remarked the practical Jack Knowles; not without an inward chuckle at the remembrance of what the speculator would have got for his money. "Was he a dealer?"

"Some sort of chap of that sort, I think. Name of Hahn. Some sort of foreigner, I should judge, though he spoke English wonderfully. He's been absolutely pestering me all the morning, and I very nearly had to kick him out. And then he came prowling about again when I had gone out, the charwoman tells me, and *she* almost had to kick him out. But anyhow, come along and try it. We'll call for Fields on the way—and Castle, if we can find him in."

The party set out forthwith, Norie and Kirk walking in front, and Knowles and Sewell, bursting with hilarious anticipation, behind them. Castle was out, and so was abandoned to his fate, but Field was found, and made up the party to five. And so the five, puffing their cigars in comfortable expectation—though of different things—left the lighted streets and took the dark road out toward the studio.

They reached and passed the first group of villas and turned into the lane; and, as they did so, Norie was startled to observe his skylight suddenly lit up from within.

"Hullo! look at that!" he cried. "And the end skylight's open! Hooray! Burglars at last!"

And he sprang off at a run, feeling for his key as he went, with the rest at his heels.

Jack Knowles sprang on the boundary wall to cut off retreat by the skylight, and Norie turned the key and flung open the door in a single movement. There was a bang and a scramble within, and there hung the terrified Hahn, by the frame of the open skylight, struggling to climb out, with one foot on a chair below, while above him appeared the grinning face of Jack Knowles!

"Hullo, Misder Hahn! Don't you got no petter vays to gollect your vines as dis?" cried Norie, with a vile attempt at a German accent. "Gom down dere, Misder Hahn!" and he seized the pallid intruder by the coat-tails and dragged him pell-mell into the middle of the room.

"Oh, forgive me, Mr. Norie, sir!" the captive pleaded, almost at a whisper, his mouth dry with terror. "I have done nothing, nothing at all, really!—and I will pay anything—anything you like! I will!"

"Oh yes, you said that this morning, you know," replied Norie. "But in mine guntry you bays six months hard for into oder beeble's houses glimbing, Misder Hahn, don't id? Sit down on der floors mit yourselfs, Misder Hahn, while I mine frients entertain," and with a quick jerk he seated the unhappy Hahn in the middle of the floor.

"Come now," Norie went on to the rest of the company, "here's more amusement than I expected to be able to give you. We'll resolve ourselves into a committee to sit on Mr. Hahn, before Mr. Hahn goes to sit in Black Maria. But first the drinks. We're going to open the Tokay, Misder Hahn, and if you like a respectable burglar yourselfs behafe, you shall see us drink it, all for nodings."

Norie went to the cupboard and brought out the magnum, and then the glasses. Knowles and Sewell, with a joyful hope of what this new complication might bring forth, laughed loud and long, now that the burglar's plight gave some excuse for their hilarity.

Norie drew the cork in a broken mass, and began pouring the stuff into the glasses. It came out a thick brown mess, and as he saw it Hahn's eyes opened wider and wider.

"Come along, you fellows," cried Norie hospitably. "Catch hold, and we'll drink Mr. Hahn's very good health, hoping the treadmill will do his liver good."

Knowles and Sewell discreetly procrastinated, but

Norie, Fields, and Kirk, suspecting nothing, took simultaneous gulps, and instantly went in a jostling rush for the fire-place, spitting and splurting the horrible mixture over the hearth. Knowles and Sewell shrieked aloud.

"Heavens! What abomination is this?" roared Norie; and as he said it his eye fell on the cowering Hahn. "Oh!" he cried, the wrong explanation dawning on him suddenly, "*this* is your game, is it? Eh? Where's *my* bottle? What have you done with the bottle you changed for this, eh?"

Hahn protested and pleaded dismally. He vowed he had made no exchange, and that the bottle then before them was the one Norie had bought.

"Oh!" exclaimed Norie, with judicial decision. "Then in that case, since you were so anxious to buy it, you shall have some for nothing—in a mug. Jack —give me that quart mug out of the cupboard!"

The mug was brought, and filled to the brim; and since the miserable Hahn would not take it at Norie's polite invitation, he was seized from behind by the elbows, and the riotous mixture of vinegar, rum, mustard, salad oil, and other fluids, was poured into his mouth, over his face and down his neck. And

when his struggles removed his mouth from easy acces-
sibility, the quart pot was inverted on his head.

But through it all, Hahn's mind was never far from
the cause of his presence in Norie's studio. It struck
him that Norie must have emptied the magnum, and
perhaps found the jewel. So as soon as the mug was
emptied, and he was momentarily released, he staggered
dripping to Norie's side and whispered hoarsely, "Share
it, and I won't say anything! You know what I could
do, but if you'll go halves I'll say nothing about it!"

"Go halves?" cried the amazed Norie. "He says
he wants to go halves! Why, you can have the lot, and
welcome! Jack, give him some more Tokay!"

And he got some more. And straightway, on the
motion of Jack Knowles, he was hauled into the street
and started on the way to the police station. The
actual distance might have been a mile and a quarter,
but the distance for Hahn was made one of galloping
leagues, by reason of his captors, taking turns in pairs,
rushing him up and down the road at top speed before them, as an instalment of prison exercise in advance.

So his torture endured, till at last, in the lighted

streets, Knowles and Sewell had charge of him well ahead of the rest, and not far from the police station. They, knowing the secret of the "Tokay," were inclined to be merciful.

"I think the poor devil's had enough," said Jack Knowles behind the prisoner's back. "We'll let him bolt down a side street, and take the fellows to the real Tokay before we tell 'em the whole sell."

And so they let him go at the next corner, with a shove and a view halloa, which brought the rest of the party on their heels.

"Gone away!" cried Jack Knowles. "But if you'll come to my place I'll give you a glass of Tokay that I prefer even to yours, Norie. Come along!"

And Harvey Crook, on his way to call on Symons at Waterview Terrace, stepped aside a moment as a panting fugitive hurried past him, and then stood to let pass a laughing group of young men, among whose voices he clearly recognised two, which were joined in a promise to the rest that the real Tokay should repair all the disappointments of the evening.

III.

MR. CLIFTON'S MAGNUM.

I.

On the evening when Hahn suffered at the hands of Mr. Norie and his friends, Mr. Symons, the auctioneer's clerk, looked out eagerly from his garden gate in Waterview Terrace, in expectation of a visit from Mr. Harvey Crook.

He was a business-like young man, this Symons, destined, no doubt, to a future partnership with his present employer. The business was growing, and more than once Symons had stopped at the opposite side of the road to judge the effect which large gilt letters would give to the style and title, "Lawson and Symons," on the office window; and no doubt it would have been a great improvement to that same window. Meantime the assiduous Symons lost no opportunity of business, and his pleasures were few and cheap.

The slaughter of snails in his little front garden and an occasional air on the flute could not be called expensive amusements, even by the very business-like and frugal wife who abetted his ambitions. And among the opportunities of business which he was resolved not to lose, this opportunity brought him by Harvey Crook was chiefly occupying his attention just now. Something had occurred to his mind during the day, and that something had led to cogitation and inquiry; and the sum of it was that he sent a note to Crook's hotel, to ask him to call at Waterview Terrace in the evening. And there he stood at the garden gate in the dark, looking out.

Crook came, a few minutes late.

"Good evening, sir," said Symons. "Would you like to step inside? My wife's out."

"Ah," replied Crook, "that sounds ungallant, now. I should have been delighted to make Mrs. Symons's acquaintance. As it is, perhaps the terrace would be as pleasant a place as anywhere—since we are to talk business."

For Crook had no desire to take risks, even remote risks, and a listening little maid-of-all-work was as likely

a part of Mr. Symons' household equipment as anything.

"It can't be called a cold night," he added.

"Very well," Symons responded, "I don't mind. Of
course you'll understand I haven't told the wife anything about this affair."

Symons was one of those men who always speak of
the wife; it is a particular sort of man, quite easy to
recognise after a little experience.

"No?" replied Crook. "Don't talk to her of business matters, I suppose?"

"Yes—in a general way; but not in detail. She
doesn't want it, you see. She has plenty of detail of
her own to look after. I may tell her about this after
it's all over, but not till then."

"Well, perhaps that will be best. I got your note.
Have you had that other collector round at the office
yet?"

"Rather!" Mr. Symons chuckled joyously. "Foreigner, I should think, but talks wonderful English.
Found him waiting at the door when I got there in the
morning. He wanted particulars of the sale of those
magnums of Tokay, of course, just as you did. I pulled

out the marked catalogue, as in duty bound, and told him what there was in it—which wasn't much good to him, as you know. And then, as a special favour, I told him that I happened to know, privately, the address of one buyer, and I gave him Mr. Norie's."

"Did that satisfy him?"

"Satisfy him? Well, I hardly know; but he rushed out of the office without another word, and when I got to the street door to look after him he was very nearly at the corner—going to Mr. Norie's!"

"Well, he won't be very successful there, I expect. But was that all you wanted to tell me? Or have you got some of the magnums for me?"

"No—not quite that. But I've found out who has one. It's old Mr. Clifton."

"And who is he?"

"Ah—of course you wouldn't know, not living here-about. He's a queer old card—a regular collector and a rare hermit. I'm pretty sure he won't sell, any more than Mr. Norie would. He buys things often enough —books and pictures, and china and bronzes to any amount, but I never heard of him selling anything yet.

6*

He had one bottle—No. 96 star in the catalogue, one of those I put no name to.   He usually pays cash."

"And you remembered the circumstance to-day?"

"Yes, in a sort of way.   Thinking it over, I had a kind of recollection that a porter got into trouble with one buyer through trying to be obliging and rolling up his bottle in a curious, dirty old hanging picture he'd bought earlier in the sale—Japanese, I think, or Chinese. A kick—kack—I forget what it is called."

"Kakemono?"

"Ah, that's it.   A dusty old thing with a tarnished gold brocade border—figure of a god or something, brown with age and smoke.   You see the porters are always anxious to see to Mr. Clifton's lots for him, be-cause he's always good for a handsome tip for any little service of that sort.   But this unlucky chap got a rare rating—though I must say the picture was dirty and ragged enough already, and most people wouldn't have given twopence for it."

"That's quite possible—and yet Mr. Clifton may have got a prize.   Rolled up in my bag at this moment there is another old kakemono which you couldn't buy for a hundred pounds."

"Indeed, sir? Well, remembering what I tell you, I turned up the marked catalogue and found that it was Mr. Clifton who had bought the kakemono. It was rather odd I didn't remember that, because he is often in at the sales. But if you are clerk of the sale you have to keep your wits on your work, and you easily forget little things like that. But the porter remembered at once when I spoke to him."

"Is Mr. Clifton a very keen buyer of rare wines?"

"Well—no, I haven't noticed that he is. But books —rare ones—china, bronzes, all things of that sort he *is* keen on. I have never been in his house—nobody has, scarcely—but they say it's piled from floor to ceiling, and still he goes on buying. Japanese and Chinese things he's very great on, they say. We don't have a great deal of that sort of stuff through our hands, of course, but whenever we catalogue a single piece he's always down to look at it. Now, as I said, I don't think he's at all likely to sell anything he has once bought, but I'll write and ask him about that magnum of Tokay, if you like."

"No," Crook replied very decidedly, "you'd better not do that. That is the very worst way in the world

to approach a man of that sort. I think the kakemono
I have will be the best possible introduction to Mr.
Clifton. Where does he live?"

"The name of the house is Downs Lodge—if you've
got a pocket-book or anything, I'll write the address
down for you. That's the name of the house, but you
won't see it stuck up anywhere. He took down the
name as soon as he came to the house, years ago—he'll
go to any lengths for privacy." Mr. Symons laughed
suddenly. "By Jove," he added, "you'll see that by
the windows—you wouldn't think the house was inhabited at all!"

"Why?"

"Dirt—dirt half an inch thick. That game began
about seven or eight years ago. You see when he took
Downs Lodge—bought it, in fact—it stood all alone in
the lane. There were fields opposite, fields behind, and
fields on each side, and that suited his solitary notions.
It isn't a very big house, but still it is of a pretty decent
size, and it's planted much nearer the roadway than
you usually see so large a house, except in the middle
of a town. He was quite happy in his solitude, till, as
I say, about seven or eight years ago, when somebody

bought the fields opposite and built a row of villas on it, and then he got very angry. Wanted to buy the villas and pull 'em down, but the chap wouldn't sell. So the old gentleman, swearing he wouldn't be pried on, gave orders that the windows weren't to be cleaned any more—at any rate outside—and they haven't been. Take a good look at the windows if you go, just for curiosity. They *are* a curiosity, I can assure you. You'd never believe such a lot of dirt could gather on a window and stick there, unless it was slapped on with a trowel. It's a licker where it all came from! It must be pretty dark inside, but nobody can see in, that's certain enough. And doesn't it just scandalise the villa residents, too. So mighty genteel! Quite destroys the 'select' character of the spot, they say!" And Mr. Symons laughed again.

Crook and the auctioneer's clerk walked a few yards in silence. "I think I know just the sort of old gentleman Mr. Clifton is," Crook remarked, at length. "Now I'd wager with all this desire for solitude, and all his other eccentricities, he's a very pleasant old fellow to speak to?"

"If you did, sir, you'd win. He's a real old gentleman—when he isn't put out. Very dignified—*very*—but treats even the office boy as courteously as you please. Even when he let out at the porter for rolling up the bottle in the picture he didn't slang him, you know—not a bit; but the poor chap looked as though he'd like to be safely in his grave!"

"Not married, I take it—remembering the dirty windows?"

"Oh no—or, at any rate, got no wife living. No, there's nobody in the house beside himself but an old cook-housekeeper and one housemaid to help her."

"Very good—I'll send him a note to-night, by hand. Mind, if that other collector calls he isn't to have this address—at any rate, not till I've done with it. Good night!"

"No, sir, of course not. He shall have no more than he's got already. Good night!"

II.

THIS was Harvey Crook's note to Mr. Clifton, despatched by messenger immediately after his return to the Royal Hotel:—

"DEAR SIR,—I am staying for a few days in Southampton, and I have chanced to hear that you are much interested in Oriental art, and a collector of fine specimens. I am only lately from the East, and I happen to have with me now a very fine and rare specimen which I think you would like to see. It is a kakemono, an authentic piece of work of the great Chinese painter of the eleventh century, Muh Ki, usually called by Europeans Mokkei, that being, as you are aware, the Japanese form of the name. I cannot say whether or not any other specimen of Mokkei's work exists in Europe, but I should think probably not. In any case, if you would care to inspect it I shall be very glad to show it you, and, if you like, bring it to your house for that purpose. I suggest this because I think it probable that you may have copies of Mokkei's works in your possession—even good copies being greatly prized, as, of course, you know—and may like to compare them. But if you would prefer to come to my hotel I will gladly keep any appointment you may make.—I am, dear sir, yours faithfully,

"HARVEY CROOK."

It was past nine o'clock when the messenger set out
with this letter, but the distance was not great, and he
was back in an hour—with an answer:—

"DEAR SIR,—I am, indeed, your debtor for so welcome
a piece of kindness as that you offer. I have never
with my own eyes beheld an original piece of work from
the hand of the divine genius Mokkei, though, as you
conjecture, I have in my collection several copies of
works of his executed by eminent Chinese and Japanese
painters of later days, reverent followers of his great
traditions; and I have seen photographs. I need
scarcely say that I shall hail the opportunity of actually
seeing and handling Mokkei's work with delight and
with gratitude to yourself. Is the picture certified in
any way?

"I trust I am not treading on delicate ground, but
if you should at any time think of disposing of the
specimen, I should much esteem an opportunity of
possessing so great a prize. If I am indiscreet in suggesting this, I trust you will pardon the natural eagerness of an ardent collector.

"Your conjecture that there may not be another

specimen of Mokkei's work in Europe is near to being correct, but not quite. There is one picture in a private collection in this country, but I have never had an opportunity of seeing it, though I am told it is very fine.

"How long do you stay in Southampton? I am prevented from seeing you early to-morrow, but if you can conveniently call here at half-past six I shall be delighted to welcome you. As you suppose, I should greatly desire to compare the Mokkei with my copies, and this is my excuse for troubling you, instead of waiting on you myself, as I should have been so glad to do. Perhaps you will let me have a note in course of to-morrow, telling me if I may expect you.

"Renewing my thanks for your kindness, I am, dear sir, yours very truly,

"BASIL CLIFTON."

So much was very satisfactory, and Harvey Crook slept with the consciousness that he had done all that prudence would allow to bring him to the third magnum of Tokay and its possibly priceless contents. The chances, of course, were increasing with each magnum.

The eleven to one chance against the Eye of Goona
being in the bottle opened on the *Rajapur* had been
decided in favour of the odds, and the one chance in
eleven—ten to one against—in the case of Mr. Norie's
magnum had also failed to come off. The chances now,
in regard to Mr. Clifton's magnum, were nine to one
against, which was no such desperate chance after all.
But the thing would have to be done with a great deal
of care. Mr. Clifton would probably be in a far calmer
mood than were the two wild young artists, Knowles
and Sewell, the night before. More, he would be a
punctilious host, which would make a vast difference.

III.

HARVEY CROOK despatched his note accepting Mr.
Clifton's invitation early the next morning. Mr. Clifton
had said nothing about dinner, but doubtless there
would be dinner, and for a moment Crook wondered
whether or not the old collector would expect him to
dress. Perhaps not, since the time fixed was so early;
and in any case the matter settled itself, for Crook had
brought no dress clothes.

He kept within walls for the best part of the day, since Hahn must be somewhere in the neighbourhood, and he saw no reason for giving that speculator notice that his erstwhile tool was a rival in the hunt. He heard of Hahn, nevertheless, for in the lunch-hour Symons came to the hotel to report that he had called at the office again.

"He looked a bit used up," Symons observed; "a bit pale and wild, and he seemed to walk stiffly. He wanted to see the marked catalogue again, so I put on the slightly offended. 'I thought I showed it to you yesterday,' I said. 'But you can see it again, of course, if you like. Hadn't you better take a copy this time?' He said he would, and he did. Then he began to pester me for addresses again. 'I told you the only one I knew yesterday,' I said. 'That was Mr. Norie's. Do you want that again?' But no, he didn't want that —the mention of it seemed to give him a sort of jump; I don't know why. So I said, 'Well, the only other names are Smith, Allen, and Curtice, and I don't know their addresses. You can find Smiths all over the town if you want 'em, and there's an Allen I can give you the address of, though whether it's the right one or not I can't say.' So I gave him the address of the only Allen I know—not the buyer, of course—and he rushed off *there*. I expect he'll have a warm reception. Allen's generally mad drunk, and always thinks a stranger is a bailiff!"

As the time neared for starting, Harvey Crook took from his kit-bag the carefully-tied roll which he had brought from London with him, and spread it out on the table before him. It was an ancient and much-damaged piece of silk, so carefully mended and rein-forced between itself and its tough paper backing that it presented a perfect network of innumerable patches when held to the light. The silk was brown with age, but on it, in Chinese ink, appeared a perfectly startling representation of a wild goose, flying, with outstretched neck, over a bed of rushes wherein its mate stood. The whole thing was done in a few bold sweeps of the brush, but, notwithstanding its faded condition and the many mendings of the nine-hundred-year-old silk, the picture gave a most amazing impression of life, vigour, and movement, and affected the mind like some living presence.

Crook dusted it carefully and re-rolled it, folding in

its outer turn, where the bordering brocade came, the ancient paper certificate of authenticity. Having done which, he sent for a cab.

The cab took the same way that Crook had taken on his walk to Norie's studio, two nights before, as far as the fork in the road. There it turned off to the left, and ran some little way among groups of small houses separated by gardens and an occasional field, before it took another turn and pulled up.

Crook stepped out, and found himself before a detached house of moderate size, standing scarcely a dozen yards back from its front railings and the road. Such small part of the garden as was visible seemed to be in very bad order; but what gave the house its distinctive look—and a very desolate look it was—were the windows. Truly Symons had not exaggerated, and it would have been difficult to believe that the house was inhabited were it not that the doorsteps, the door, the knocker, and its other fittings were clean and bright, in almost uncanny contrast to the rest of the housefront—like a smiling eye in a dead face.

Crook paid his fare, pushed through the iron gate, which creaked aloud, mounted the steps, and placed his hand on the bell-pull. He did not ring, for at that moment the door opened.

The contrast of the door with the grimy windows was more than maintained by the hall. It was large, and clean, and cheerful, furnished with old oak, and spread with a Persian rug. On the rug stood a thin, grizzled man of about fifty-five, bowing and smiling.

"How do you do, Mr. Crook?" asked the smiling man, extending his hand. "I am Mr. Clifton. I heard your cab, and I came to the door myself. Pray come in. My housekeeper, unfortunately, is just taken rather unwell, and the housemaid, my only other servant, has her evening out. Let me take your hat. The absence of the housemaid, I fear, is wholly due to my own carelessness. I said nothing to my housekeeper about your visit till an hour ago, when the housemaid was already gone. But no doubt you will pardon any little inconvenience—you are so very kind to come. And is this the precious parcel?"

It was growing dark outside, and here in the hall a lamp was necessary. It had been already lighted when Crook entered, and now his host took it up and led the way past the staircase end.

"The library is rather in confusion, and I fear the fire is out," he said. "I think we shall be more comfortable in the dining-room. There is just one step here—be careful."

Everywhere the house was most handsomely furnished, and the walls were hung close and thick with pictures. The dining-room looked large and sombre in the single light of the lamp, but very speedily candles were lit on the mantelpiece, and in a large chandelier, and a very handsome room was disclosed. A set of early Georgian chairs, with elegantly carved backs, stood about a many-legged dining table of the same period, and elsewhere the room was a medley of books, pictures, and bric-a-brac.

"It's really almost the only decently-habitable room I have," said the master of the house, as he set down the lamp at last. "True, there is confusion enough here; but in the other rooms a stranger could not step without causing some terrible damage."

"I have heard that your collections are very large," Crook remarked.

"Enormous! Enormous—I mean, of course, for the size of the house. And all in the most admired dis-

order, I give you my word, Mr. Crook. You may observe that I say 'admired disorder' and *not* 'admired
confusion,' as the words are so commonly misquoted. I
cannot bear to hear a classic misused. But there, that
is not our business to-night, after all! I need not say
I am all impatience to see the—ah—the specimen!"

Harvey Crook took the wrappings from his precious
roll and spread out the ancient picture tenderly on the
polished table. Looking up suddenly as he did so, he
was not a little surprised to note that his host's eyes, instead of being directed eagerly on the spread silk, were
turned toward the door of the room, rather with the expression of a man who intently listens than that of one
who looks.

"There it is, Mr. Clifton," Crook said; "and this is
the certificate I had with it."

The other's eyes came quickly back to the table.
"Ah, precisely," he said. "Precisely. A very wonderful and interesting specimen, to be sure. And the
certificate also—Chinese, I see. I am really infinitely
obliged to you, Mr. Crook—quite infinitely obliged to
you."

This connoisseur's manner puzzled Harvey Crook.

Where was the passionate enthusiasm, the delighted wonder, that Mr. Clifton's letter had led him to expect as a matter of course? The words were the polite words of one who is expected to admire something that fails to interest him; though certainly they were delivered with much emphasis and a tone of great warmth.

"I got it in China," Crook explained, "at Soochow. It was an exchange for some manuscript that I knew I couldn't sell anywhere else. A Japanese expert thought a vast deal of it. You know, of course, that in Japan the work of the ancient Chinese painters is more highly prized than in China itself."

"Indeed? Oh yes, of course—yes, certainly, so it is. Very extraordinary, isn't it? You know I can't tell you how immensely obliged I am to you for showing me this, Mr. Crook, really!"

"You mentioned some copies you had, which you wished to compare. Perhaps———"

"Ah—of course, so I did. I had almost forgotten. We'll just———what was that?"

He stood stock still, his face pallid, his palm raised,

his eyes directed toward the door, listening intently. There was a faint stir somewhere in the house—below.

"It must be the cat," he said, with an obvious effort. "Yes, the cat must have come in. Will you excuse me for one moment? I feel sure it was the cat."

He took the lamp and went out. Truly this rusty, grizzled man was a great oddity, a person of curious moods. All the enthusiasm of yesterday seemed to have vanished, and even his memory of his own letter seemed defective. Crook wondered how best he might bring the conversation to the matter of the Tokay. As yet nothing had been said about dinner—a thing which might give opportunities.

The grey man was gone for some little time, and returned at last with a more composed countenance.

"It was the cat," he said, "as I supposed. You were saying—something—oh yes, something about my copies. Well now, I think we shall find them somewhere in the drawing-room—or what would be the drawing-room, if I kept such a place. Will you come? Perhaps you will bring the—the specimen with you."

He took up the lamp once more, and Crook followed him with the old kakemono. The drawing-room was large, and far fuller of everything—furniture, pictures, china, bronzes—than the dining-room. The grey man turned to a large cabinet, and pulled open its doors.

"Unlocked, fortunately," he said. "As a matter of fact I was having a little hunt for my keys when you arrived, and I am particularly anxious to find them soon, for other reasons. Here are the—well, the specimens, you know."

The cabinet drawers were full of rolled pictures, Chinese and Japanese, and the grey man wandered among them, unrolling first one and then another, but never coming upon anything that might be considered a copy of Mokkei.

"I am afraid my things are in sad confusion," he said. "Though, of course, this is nothing to the confusion I should suffer from if I kept more servants. I find it a great advantage to keep the establishment so low that they have barely time to do the necessary work of the household, without interfering with my beloved litter. But the windows are a sad affliction to my excellent housekeeper! You noticed the windows? Of course you did—everybody does. By-the-bye, speaking of my housekeeper, if you will pardon me once more, I should much like to see how the worthy soul is getting on. She has these little attacks sometimes, but she usually recovers before long. Do you mind? Perhaps you can amuse yourself with the—specimens till I return."

He was gone a little longer this time. The carpets were soft, but Crook's ears were sharp, and he fancied that his host had gone no farther than to a door a few yards away.

As Crook sat and waited in the dimly-lit room, a large black cat came purring in at the door, stared at him full-eyed for some few moments, and then retreated behind a pile of portfolios. Just then there was a sound from some neighbouring room—slight, but noticeable in that still house. It might have been the sound of a breaking stick.

Almost immediately the smiling grey man came back.

"I really must beg a thousand pardons," he said. "But you understand my awkward situation, don't you? The poor old soul is a little better, but still far from well. You didn't hear any unusual noise, did you?"

Crook was beginning to answer when a shadow

crossed the door-opening at the grey man's side, and he turned with a gasp of terror.

"What—what's that?" he exclaimed, almost in a whisper. "The cat—it *is* the cat!"

And, indeed, it was the cat, which, encouraged to emerge from its retreat by his more familiar presence, had approached him from behind. The grey man seized one of the precious rolls of painted silk and struck savagely at the creature, which dodged and turned and sprang off into the dark corridor. The grey man turned to Crook again.

"I am growing sadly nervous of late," he said, "and a very little thing affects me. You must forgive my little eccentricities. I was speaking of my housekeeper—the good soul insisted that something must be done to offer you refreshment. I have to ask your pardon for so many things to-night that I am sure you will overlook any shortcomings in this respect. There is a cold fowl in the larder, and if you will return to the dining-room I think I will do myself the pleasure of acting host and waiter together."

It seemed that this odd person had already ceased to be interested in the painting which Crook had brought, so now nothing remained but to approach the matter of the Tokay, just as dinner might give the opportunity. So Crook made the feeblest possible protest that common politeness would permit, and followed his host back into the dining-room.

There he sat in the brilliant light of the many candles while the grey man carried the lamp to and fro between dining-room and kitchen, and so set before him the materials of a very decent cold dinner.

"As to wine now," asked the grey man presently, "what are your preferences? I think I can give you almost anything you may fancy, including some exceptionally rare vintages. I do not collect wines with the same assiduity which I devote to other things, but I have had some pieces of luck now and again."

Here was an opportunity. "Yes," assented Crook, "I heard of one such piece of luck when I was told of your liking for oriental art. They told me that you bought a kakemono at Lawson's the other day, and at the same sale were lucky enough to secure one magnum of very old Imperial Tokay."

"Ah, yes — the Tokay!" The grey man's eyes lighted up as from the sudden suggestion of a valuable idea. "The Tokay! How lucky you should remind me. We will open it, Mr. Crook. Come, I will bring it at once!"

Here was another curious thing. This connoisseur of Eastern art, yesterday learned and enthusiastic on the subject of ancient Chinese paintings and to-day almost ignorant of them, careful even to avoid their very names, was now betraying a curious ignorance as a connoisseur of wines. For who would think of drinking old Imperial Tokay with his food, instead of after? But Crook had his object to gain, and was not disposed to be critical.

Presently his new acquaintance returned with the magnum—not carrying it tenderly at a proper slope, as one who understood wines, but grasping it upright by the neck.

"Here it is," he said, putting it down on the table with a jar that would have torn the nerves of a true judge of old wines; "and since it pleases you, I am sorry I did not get more, for it was quite cheap."

He took a corkscrew from the sideboard, and essayed to open the bottle. But now Crook was surprised to perceive that his hands, steady enough for less exact work, were trembling so that he stabbed seal and cork-screw together half-a-dozen times without hitting the centre.

"Let me try," suggested Crook, jumping at the opportunity. "My hands are particularly steady, and an old wine like this needs especially careful handling."

His host yielded bottle and corkscrew gladly, and Crook saw that the seal was old and dirty and quite unbroken. He screwed and pulled the tender old cork with the greatest care, and just managed to fetch it away entire, though crumbling.

"Such an old cork needs a very steady hand," Crook said. "Have you some spare decanters?"

Decanters were found, and here, in far different circumstances, Crook began to repeat his performance of two nights ago in Norie's studio. He turned his back towards where the grey man was sitting, lifted the magnum to the light, and poured slowly.

The decanters were fairly large, and two sufficed to hold the contents of the magnum. Steadily, slowly, Crook filled the first, and saw no sign of the great jewel that was leading his quest. Slowly and steadily he filled the second, watching and watching, and no Green

Eye came to the neck. The matter was settled. The
Green Eye of Goona was not in Mr. Clifton's magnum.

Crook put the second decanter on the table, and
turned to make the best of his dinner. He found a
large hock glass by his plate, and no other.

"This is indeed a generous glass for Tokay," he
said, and half filled it.

Indeed the wine was far too sweet for a dinner
wine, but Crook made the best of it. Surely no man
would be so ungracious as to grumble at this lavish use
of so noble and rare a liquor in his honour, and Crook,
his turn served and his work done, applied himself to
the meal. His freakish host was agreeable and
sedulous, though through it and with it all Crook felt
the discomfort of some odd prepossession, some inex-
plicable constraint. Truly this was an odd fellow, and
for all his politeness, in some strange way not altogether
an agreeable fellow.

"Bless me!" he exclaimed presently, "I thought I
had remembered everything, but I observe I have forgotten the cheese. Odd I should have forgotten the
cheese! I have a Stilton of which I really think you
will approve." He rose and turned about, and then

added suddenly, "No, no, I am wrong—here it is on the console table. Come, I hope you will like the Stilton. Meantime, as I do not take cheese, is it asking too much to beg you to excuse me once more? I am really anxious about that good soul, my housekeeper. Pray do not spare the wine."

Again Crook was left alone, and he turned to the cheese, which was, in fact, excellent. The house was still—curiously still. But as he sat he presently heard again that same slight cracking noise, as of a stick or some wooden thing broken and splintered, away in some far room, behind thick doors and curtains. And in a few minutes more the sound was repeated.

Harvey Crook sat in solitude, sipping his wine and listening for the return of his host. But the silence of that strange house was unbroken. Once he fancied he heard a slight creak from the outer gate—possibly caused by the wind.

Presently the black cat came in, cautiously, tentatively, waiting for a moment to gaze at him from the door, and so judge of what reception to expect. Crook took a fragment from his plate to tempt the animal, and it came, cautiously still, stood a yard away, and mewed. Crook dropped the fragment, and the cat ate it and came closer.

Still he sat solitary, and there was no sound from end to end of the house. Some of the candles began to gutter down, and he rose and blew these out. The cat followed him.

It began to grow late. What should he do? Politeness dictated that he should wait for his host, but everything earthly has its limit. He stood and looked at a picture on the wall, and the cat rubbed against his legs, purring.

The picture hung on the wall opposite the door, which stood ajar. Crook fancied some cold waft of wind from without, walked to the door, opened it, and peered into the dark beyond. The cat came after him again, purring.

The house beyond the dining-room was black and silent, but a cool fresh wind came along the corridor as though an outer door were open. Should he do anything to remind his host of his presence? If the housekeeper were worse, perhaps he might be of use, to call a doctor, or the like. He ventured a loud cough.

The sound went through the house with startling clearness, and through the tense quiet a dozen tiny echoes came whispering back. But that was all.

He stepped into the corridor, and pronounced aloud the name of the master of the house; and again there was no answer but the whispering echoes.

He returned to the dining-room and took a candle from the mantelpiece. Right or wrong, he would see what this thing meant.

Candle in hand, he strode along the corridor, the cat trotting at his heels. As he came into the hall, his light met a gust of air which nearly blew it out. The front door was open!

He pushed it to, stood by the stair-foot and called aloud, "Mr. Clifton! Mr. Clifton!" And again the house gave back no living voice.

Behind the main staircase a smaller staircase descended, half hidden by a curtain which seemed to have lately been partly torn from its rings. The torn curtain thus having taken his eye, Crook stepped toward it and descended the stairs.

It was a short flight, for the basement floor was low-ceiled. At the bottom he could see the kitchen door, half shut, and jammed against some indistinct object—a bundle of clothes, perhaps—on the floor.

Crook held the light aloft and pushed the door wide open, and there lay the bundle of clothes—a woman: a stout, neatly-dressed woman with her head beaten out of human recognition!

What was this—the housekeeper? The housekeeper of whose welfare her master had been so solicitous? The cat looked up from between Crook's legs and mewed plaintively.

He turned and dashed up the stairs, for it came on him overwhelmingly that this was not the bottom of the mystery. He pushed open one door and another, and found all dark and silent. Then a third, and light streamed out—lamplight and firelight: the library.

Books—the books were everywhere, from floor to ceiling and over the floor. But to Harvey Crook's eyes the room seemed even less full of books than of blood—dripping, sticking, smeared, and ghastly. And in the midst of it all, lolling horribly in a chair, from which only the table's edge kept him from sliding, was a man, a handsome, white-haired old man, dabbled and terrible, with his head back, and a fearful gash across his throat.

A small safe, let into the wall, was standing open, and the little iron drawers from within it were tumbled on the floor. Across the room stood a writing-table, of which all the drawers but two had been forced open; and, as he saw this, Crook remembered the cracking noises he had heard, and remembered how the grey man had complained of the loss of his keys. While here, he knew now, lay Mr. Basil Clifton, dead in his blood, while he, Crook, had been sitting at table with his murderer!

Harvey Crook ran out at the front door, and beat at the knockers of the villas opposite. What followed he never afterwards remembereed with much distinctness. Women fainted, men were white in the face, and after a time there was a returning servant girl, hysterical and screaming. Then the police came, and he was told that for the present he must consider himself in custody; and that cleared his faculties.

IV.

HARVEY CROOK'S arrest was not a long one, and after certain explanations and an hour or two's detention he was allowed to return to his hotel, though he had more than a suspicion that he was still under observation. But at the inquest the whole matter was made plain, partly by the testimony of the housemaid, partly by other evidence. The vanished murderer was one James Pritchard, a friend of Mr. Clifton's in early youth. In middle life affairs had gone ill with him, he had made efforts to repair them in which the practice of forgery was involved, and penal servitude was his punishment. Mr. Clifton had strongly upheld his innocence, and, now that he was released, had begun to employ him temporarily to catalogue his library, while some more permanent employment might be looked for; and this was the end of it all. The ungrateful wretch had murdered his benefactor and the housekeeper, the only other person in the place, for the sake of whatever he might find in the safe.

It was not so very much, after all—sixty or seventy pounds in notes and gold, so far as could be ascertained. It became plain that the crime must have been committed just before Harvey Crook's arrival, and that it was only on turning over his victim's papers that the murderer learned that Crook was expected, and became acquainted with the reason of his call. Before he could find the keys with which the safe might be opened Crook arrived, and in order to gain time to gather his plunder unmolested, Pritchard had adopted the expedient of himself posing as Mr. Clifton. Harvey Crook was young, strong, and alert, or possibly the wretch might have made a further attempt on him. At it was he contrived to escape from his guest's company from time to time, break open the drawers of the writing-table till he had found the safe keys, and at last decamp with what plunder he could secure. It turned out, afterward, that the keys which would have enabled him to open the writing-table without trouble were in a pocket of a waistcoat of Mr. Clifton's hanging under a heap of other clothes in a press in his dressing-room.

So much Harvey Crook learned, with the rest of the world, at the inquest. But he had not learned all, nor even all that concerned himself and his search.

———

IV.

THE STEWARD'S MAGNUM—AND ANOTHER.

I.

So far we have followed Harvey Crook in his quest of the scattered magnums of Tokay and what some one of them might contain beside the wine. We now return to the scatterer of those magnums—Mr. Lyman W. Merrick, of Merricksville, Pennsylvania — and his daughter Daisy.

When he—and his daughter, quite as important as her father in other beside his own fatherly eyes—had bid good-bye to Harvey Crook: when the sale was over, and Mr. Merrick had calculated that his one bottle of Tokay had cost him nine hundred and seventy-five dollars, while he had sold eleven other bottles at two or three dollars apiece: and when he had slept over the adventure, father and daughter spent a day in seeing what could be seen in the time from Southampton—Portsmouth and the *Victory* in particular. And at the end of that day they dined together in a private room of the hotel which was to cater for their one remaining night in Southampton.

Somehow, it was not an extremely lively dinner. In point of fact both were a little dull. It is possible that Mr. Merrick somewhat regretted the Tokay. He was lavish enough with his money, but he had a considerable dislike to looking foolish, and he had something more than a vague idea that he looked a little foolish over this transaction of the wine—at any rate to himself. He rather wished, now, that he had kept it. There would have been drawbacks, of course. A great case of a dozen magnums of precious wine would have been a sad encumbrance in the pursuit of the express-rate tour which he and Daisy designed for themselves; there would have been constant anxiety as to breakages —and probably there would have been the actual breakages also. Still, he wished he had kept, at any rate, a single magnum for himself, and put some sort of reserve price on the rest.

As for Daisy, she also was a trifle less vivacious

than usual.   Perhaps when one has been in daily
acquaintance with a few pleasant people in the narrow
confines of a steamship for best part of a month, it is
a little depressing to lose them all suddenly, and find
oneself in a hotel where everybody is strange; perhaps
one is none the less dull when one of the friends who
have gone is a pleasant and entertaining man of thirty-
five — Harvey Crook was entertaining and pleasant;
also thirty-five.   Thirty-five is quite young, nowadays,
for a man.   Not that that mattered, of course.   Why
should it?

Mr. Merrick alluded to the subject of his own
thoughts; Daisy said nothing about the subject of
hers.   Coffee was brought, and Mr. Merrick lit a
cigar.

"Well, Daisy," he said, "I guess I shall have to do
without a glass of Tokay this time."

"Are you only just beginning to regret your speculation, father?" asked Daisy.   You will observe that,
although she was an American young lady, she did not
say "popper," or "pop," or "paw."   That was because
she had a sense of humour, and saw no reason for
making both herself and her father ridiculous.

"Well," that gentleman answered, "I suppose no man would be over and above high-and-mighty satisfied with a speculation that lost him thirty-nine fortieths of his stake, *as* a speculation. But I was thinking it might ha' been as well to keep one magnum anyway— just as a curiosity. It mightn't have been altogether a mistake to ha' kept the lot. It would ha' come in pretty handy for presents when we got back—a bottle here and there of such a wine as that would ha' been thought considerable of, I believe—'specially if I let the price leak out sort of accidental. But, anyway, I don't mind confessing, right here, that I do wish I'd kept one bottle."

"Well, father," suggested Daisy with something of a twinkle, "perhaps there wouldn't be any great difference between dropping thirty-nine fortieths of that thousand dollars and dropping all the forty?"

"No, there wouldn't. A bottle of wine costs nine hundred and seventy-five dollars or a thousand — no such mighty difference. But why?"

"Because I think it's pretty likely you can get a bottle back for the other twenty-five dollars. That

would bring the price down to five hundred dollars each
for the pair, wouldn't it?"

"There's nothing the matter with the arithmetic,"
her father answered doubtfully, "but the wine's pretty
well out of reach by this time, I guess."

"But *surely* you remember who bought the very first
magnum put up for sale?"

"Why, yes, of course—the steward of the *Rajapur;*
and pretty much of a startler I got when I heard the
price he got it for."

"Well, father, if you were in the habit of watching
people as closely as I do, you'd guess that McNab
didn't buy that wine to drink himself. He speculated;
but he's a pretty hard-headed sort of Scotchman, and
he'll make more of his speculation than you did, father!
But you can buy his bottle, I'm sure, if he hasn't sold
it already."

"Come," cried her father, "that's a notion! We'll
send and find him."   And he rang for the waiter.

Duncan McNab, chief steward of the *Rajapur,* was
a methodical man of business, and he was not difficult
to find that evening. The *Rajapur,* because of its accident, was to stay at Southampton for repairs before

proceeding to London. Mr. McNab had seen the
passengers off, and collected whatever contributions were
forthcoming, the day before, and had also found time
to come ashore and make his little speculation. He
had rather expected to see the Tokay go cheap. All
this following day he had not been idle, and he was
busy with his accounts when he received Mr. Merrick's
message. He curbed some natural resentment at being
disturbed by a person who was no longer a passenger,
and consequently no concern of his, by the reflection
that possibly Merrick had repented of his disastrous
transaction in wine, and now wished to recover at least
one of his lost magnums; a perfectly accurate conjecture, as we have seen. For some hours the frugal soul
of McNab had been troubled by a fear that perhaps he
had foolishly risked his money—the magnum had cost
him nine shillings—after all, and that he might wait for
long ere he found anybody sufficiently daft to pay him
a profit on his purchase. But at the hint of the
message he took his hat, tightened his lips, and set his
face toward the hotel.

"Ou ay," quoth the McNab doubtfully, when he had
listened to Mr. Merrick's explanation of his message.

The steward spoke with a sourly thoughtful air, as though the suggestion of selling his property struck him as an unwelcome encroachment on his rights. "Ou ay; ha—hum; hum. A'm thinkin' ye'll ken that buyin' an' sellin' is aye twa deeferent things."

"That," said Mr. Merrick, "is a piece of wisdom which this wine transaction would have taught me already, I guess, if I had never heard of it before."

"Ou ay. Weel, an' what might ye be thinkin' of offering for the bottle of wine? 'Tis a muckle big bottle."

"The same size as the others, of course. You gave nine shillings for it; I guess it's your business to say what profit you want on that."

"Ha, hum. 'Twas circulatit aboard that ye paid twa hoondred poond for the twal' bottles. Noo, that wad mak' the bottle ye drinkit come to ower a hoondred an' ninety-five poond. Weel, noo, I'll no ask ye as much as that for mine."

"I'd call that a mighty wise judgment, steward," replied Mr. Merrick solemnly. "Unless you want to keep it for yourself?"

No; McNab obviously did not want to keep the magnum for himself. But his notion of the price was presently seen to be just the very highest sum that could be squeezed out of the purchaser, and his opinion of his present customer's squeezability was a very exalted one, to begin with. But it sank gradually, as it became plain to the steward that the American would stand no more big figures; and, in the end, with much protest, the magnum became Mr. Merrick's again for five pounds. Whereupon it became plain that the business-like McNab had come prepared to clinch the bargain on the spot, and so give the purchaser no time for repentance, for he fetched the bottle from the hotel office downstairs, where it had been lying during the interview.

So McNab went back to his ship much relieved in mind, while Mr. Merrick carefully packed away the magnum in the middle of a trunk, surrounded by clothes.

II.

FROM Southampton the Merricks made straight for London by an early train the next morning; and almost the first place they visited, as soon as they had gained the Langham Hotel and their luncheon, was the *Times* newspaper office, where Daisy's father paid for this advertisement:—

If MR. BASIL CLIFTON will communicate his present address to Lyman W. Merrick, Langham Hotel, London, he will give the advertiser the opportunity of renewing an old acquaintance, and of personally expressing his gratitude for a great act of kindness done him twenty-six years ago, in America. Any information of Mr. Clifton's whereabouts will be gratefully received.

"I'm easier in my mind after that," Merrick observed to his daughter as their cab drove away from the office. "I've tried considerable before, and I think that's about the only thing left to do. Very likely I shan't hear, but if I don't hear to-morrow, every paper in London shall have that advertisement the next day."

"I think, perhaps," Daisy suggested, looking sidelong at her father, "Mr. Clifton may not want to see you. You've written before."

"Often; but I owe him all I have, all the same, and I'm missing no chances if I can help it. Perhaps he's dead, of course—he was as old as I am now twenty-six years ago. But perhaps he isn't, and perhaps *his* luck has gone down while mine has gone up. If it has—

well I'm here to sort of make things even. It's all his, I reckon, in a way of speakin'—all from the beginning. I did nothing but sit and take what came of it."

"He lent you the money to start, didn't he, father?"

"He did—and he was a stranger. It was rather an odd trade altogether, and it was a rare piece of gall on my part to put it to him. I never told you, I think, but your poor mother knew it all, and she never let up on urging me to pay back somehow. You see, he was a great collector of all sorts of strange and curious things, and—hey gee! Why, that's just the thing!"

"What?"

"Why, the Tokay; I was just thinking. If I find him, that bottle of Tokay's just the sort of little present that 'ud please him! I ought to ha' thought o' that before! What a fool thing it was to sell the others— one magnum's no sort of a present for such a man, even a magnum of old Tokay!"

"I'm sure he'd appreciate it, whatever it was, father, if he's the sort of man you say."

"Oh yes, he would; he was a white man right through and up an' down an' all. Well, as I was say-

ing, he was a great collector of all sorts of rarities, and
at that time I had a complete Indian's rig-out of wampum—the real shell stuff—that I had brought from
West when I was a boy. Your gran'father traded an
old gun for it. Well, at that time, although it was a
sort of curio, there was no particular big money in such
a thing—a few dollars, perhaps—and it was about all
I had in the world after what clothes I stood up in.
But I was a hustling young fellow, and I had my eye—
both eyes—hard on some land—the land where Merricksville is now, my dear. The land was cheap enough,
but cheapness ain't much good to a man without a
cent, anyway, and I was most powerful set on having
that land. You can guess why, now, knowing what you
do. They'd been drawing oil in Pennsylvania for some
few years then, but there wasn't a well within sixty
miles of this place. I knew oil was there, though, and
there I stuck, pretty considerable dancin' mad to think
that here was my fortune being lost for a matter of
five hundred dollars or so. You see, it was no good a
slouch like me going around to borrow five hundred
dollars without security, and if I let on what I was
after, well, anyone that believed my judgment would

get the land for himself, of course. Well, that was how it was when I ran up against Mr. Basil Clifton.

"He was just travelling, you see—been round the world, like ourselves now, but doing it a deal slower. He wanted to see some good wampum —wanted to buy it; and somehow somebody remembered me—I was doing odd chores on a farm. He saw the set, and, as I say, he offered to buy it. Well, the only money that was any use to me just then was five hundred dollars, and the few dollars that wampum was worth—then—would ha' been no use at all. I was pretty desp'rate for that five hundred dollars, knowing what it meant, and I went in baldheaded on this chance, without much hope of getting it. 'Stranger,' I said, 'here's the stuff, as you see, but it ain't for sale. Not for sale, you see, but I'll give it for interest on a loan. I want five hundred dollars for a start in life, and I'll give this in advance for interest.'

"He opened his eyes a bit at this, but he was quite English and quiet about it. 'How long do you want that loan for?' he asked. 'Six months,' I said, 'though I guess I could pay in three.' 'I expect to be in England long before the end of three months,' he said.

'Then I should have to mail it on,' I answered. 'Any
security?' he asked. 'No,' says I. He seemed considerable amused in his quiet sort of way—he was a
man twice my age at that time, you see—and he looked
from me to the wampum and back again several times.
'Well,' he said at last, 'I'll speculate on your honour,
young man. Come to my hotel and you shall have the
money.' And I had it; and in two months the oil was
coming up in millions of gallons, and Merricksville was
begun. He'd left his banker's address, and there the
money went, under the three months, with a letter for
him. I got an answer on plain notepaper, headed care
of the bankers—a very kind answer, full of congratula-
tions—but he wouldn't take a cent more than his due;
the speculation was my own idea, he said, and he'd
already got more than the loan was worth. And then
—well then I married your mother, and got took up
with one thing and another, and it was ten years before
I wrote again. And then he'd changed his bankers,
and so I lost track of him. But I felt sort o' guilty
about it somehow, not having written for ten years, and
having made such a pile on his money, and I tried and
tried again but got no nearer. I was over here once,

as you know, and I chanced to meet an old friend of his, but he hadn't seen him for years—ever since he lost his wife and shut himself away in the country, he said. Of course, after all time, it's likely he's dead—he'd be pretty late in the seventies by this time, I guess. But I'd like to see him once again, and that's a fact!"

Now it was no more than twenty-four hours since Merrick *had* seen Mr. Basil Clifton, as we have seen, when that collector bought a magnum of the very wine he was selling. But the purchase was for cash and no name was given, neither man was thinking of the other at the moment, and even if this had not been the case the twenty-six years which had elapsed since their one and only meeting had sufficiently disguised both to prevent anything like recognition. It was one of the narrow chances that mock man's wishes a score of times in a life.

The rest of the day went in the sights of London, and the day after that. There was no answer to the advertisement.

Just before dinner on this second day in London Merrick telephoned to an advertising agency to have the notice repeated in every London paper on the following morning. And if, as Daisy Merrick sat at dinner in the Langham Hotel, she gave a thought to Harvey Crook (which she did) not her wildest dream could have pictured him as and where he was. For this was the evening of his visit to Downs Lodge.

At breakfast in the morning Merrick examined the newspapers with some interest, for he had felt some doubt as to whether his order for the advertisement had not been given too late in the day. He was reassured to perceive that his message duly had its place in each paper, and turned the news pages of the last he had examined. One thing and another he passed casually till he came to a paragraph which set him positively gasping. This was the paragraph:—

GHASTLY DOUBLE MURDER AT SOUTHAMPTON.

A double murder of an unusually horrible character was committed last night at Downs Lodge, near Southampton, a detached house in the occupation of Mr. Basil Clifton, the victims being Mr. Clifton himself and his housekeeper, Mary Carr. Robbery appears to have been the motive of the crime, as the drawers of a writing-table in Mr. Clifton's library were found broken, and a small safe had been opened. Mr. Clifton's body was found in this room, with the throat cut so deeply as almost to sever the head from the body. The housekeeper's body was found in the kitchen doorway, the unfortunate woman having evidently been killed by repeated blows on the head from some blunt instrument, probably after the attack on her master. The housemaid, the only other servant, was out for the evening when the crime was committed. A man of gentlemanly appearance, a stranger in the district, giving the name of Harvey Crook, is in custody in connection with the affair.

Here, indeed, was something to make Merrick gasp, and more. His benefactor, his once-seen friend of twenty-six years ago, long sought since, was discovered at last, butchered in his chair—and Harvey Crook was charged with the murder! They had bidden good-bye to Crook four days before, and he had started, ostensibly, for London. But here he was in Southampton again and——!

But if the effect of the news was startling on Mr. Lyman Merrick, on his daughter it was infinitely distressing. She broke into vehement protests that Crook must be innocent, insisted that they must go instantly and support his defence somehow—and then fainted while dressing to go. The end of it was that they missed the 10.15 train and went by the eleven o'clock. A fortunate circumstance after all, for, before the train left, Waterloo station was fluttering with the halfpenny

9*

evening papers which come out in the morning; the
placards flamed the Southampton murders in the biggest
capitals; and in the papers themselves, which Mr. Merrick bought by the handful, it was reported that Harvey
Crook had been released and that search was being
made for somebody else. The effect of this intelligence on Daisy Merrick, albeit tranquillising in the end,
was at first such that Lyman W. Merrick began
to regard his daughter as a very eccentric young
woman.

III.

No young lady could have been more properly self-
possessed than Daisy Merrick by the time Southampton
was reached, and when her father began to "hustle
around" in that town in search of Harvey Crook and
whatever information was to be obtained, she hustled
with him, every yard. It was not a very difficult thing
to find Crook—everybody was full of the tale of the
murders, and the police directed the searchers to his
hotel at once.

Harvey Crook was in the last stages of lunch when his visitors arrived, and Merrick rushed at him with both hands outstretched.

"Mr. Crook," he cried, "tell me what all this means! Who did it? How was it? Where were you in it? Did you know him? How—— But there, I guess you think I'm flighty under the hat. Here, look at that —it's quicker'n telling you!"

He snatched a newspaper from his pocket and pointed to his own advertisement in the "agony" column. "Do you happen to have seen that?" he asked. "My advertisement, Mr. Crook—mine!"

Crook had not seen it, and was vastly astonished to read it now. Daisy watched him with shining eyes as he read it, but she was quiet and self-possessed enough by this time.

"Why," said Crook, "this is amazing! The poor old gentleman was a friend of yours, then?"

"The friend I owe my bottom cent to, and my top cent, and all the cents in between!" exclaimed Merrick. "And I only saw him once in my life."

"That's odder still. I had a letter from him after I left you, and dined at his house last night, and yet I

never saw him till he was dead!   It seems to me that
we are all in a strange adventure together.   Sit down.
We must compare notes."

Mr. Merrick told his side of the tale sufficiently
clearly in a dozen hurried sentences, and was urgent to
know what Harvey Crook had to tell.

"My tale will take a trifle longer to explain," Crook
began.   "You and I and poor old Mr. Clifton are a
little more tangled up together than you think.   Now
listen.   When I sold you that dozen magnums of old
Tokay on board the *Rajapur,* you paid two hundred
pounds, and thought it a high price.   So did I."

"It was an almighty high price, I guess."

"No, it wasn't.   It may not have been quite so
cheap as your hundred pounds' worth of land in
Pennsylvania, twenty-six years ago, but it was the next
best bargain of your life.   In that case, Mr. Merrick,
you bought, for two hundred pounds, a few gallons of
old Tokay worth—well, that's difficult to guess, and
doesn't matter; you bought a few gallons of old Tokay
and a diamond worth all the Tokay in the world a dozen
times over!"

"*A* diamond!" ejaculated Lyman W. Merrick.

And, "*A* diamond!" cried Daisy, forgetting her English accent for the moment.

"Not only *a* diamond," Crook went on with a slight smile, "but *the* diamond—the green diamond. You remember the shindy about the Green Eye of Goona?"

"Yes," exclaimed father and daughter together, breathlessly, "at the Durbar!"

"Well, that is the jewel that was in that case of wine, and that is the jewel that you sold by auction here at Lawson's, for eight or ten shillings or so, bottle of wine included!"

"But what—why—was it in the bottle?"

"In one of the bottles—which bottle I am trying to find out. That is my business just at present, and I am very nearly as keen about that as you were about the five-hundred-dollar lot of land twenty-six years ago; for it probably means a little fortune if I am successful."

"A *little* fortune? Well, I'd guess——"

"Oh yes—the thing itself is worth something enormous, of course,—king's ransom, Jew's eye, mint of money— just whatever phrase you like to use. The only difficulty would be to find a customer for such a thing. But it's stolen property, you know."

"Stolen property? Well, yes, I guess that's about the size of it. But then it's a bit above likely that it's been stolen property any time these thousand years— stolen one way or another. That's the way with those Indian diamonds, I guess?"

"You are right, no doubt, but no matter how long it may have been stolen property, I think I'd rather not be one of the thieves. No; if I find this, it goes back to the Rajah of Goona—on terms, of course. That's where I expect to find my little fortune—just the pursuit of my trade, you see, Mr. Merrick! I find something here cheap and I sell it dear in India—or rather, I charge for risk and carriage!"

"But now I don't know—how did——"

"How it got to the bottle, exactly, I can't tell yet; but it's pretty certain that the man who put it in was Hahn, the fellow I told you of, who got me to bring the wine to England—to save the risk he feared, as I see well enough now. And, to add another interest to the chase, he's after the bottles now, in competition with me! Lord! what a taking he was in when he found I'd sold the wine!"

"And to think!—Great Scott, Mr. Crook—to think

of the fool thing I did when I shoved off them magnums at a couple o' dollars each or so! But I've got one back; I didn't tell you that. I changed my mind and bought one back the very same night!"

"Where is it?"

"It's in London at the 'Langham'—safe enough in the middle of a trunk, locked tight. Great thunder! The diamond may be in that! And McNab——" but here Merrick broke into a fit of laughter in the midst of his wonder.

"McNab? What? The chief steward? What——?"

"Lord, Mr. Crook, it's the very greatest sort of an amusement to think of the face of McNab, if ever he hears he has sold that diamond for five pounds! The very greatest!" And Merrick told the story of the recovery of the first magnum sold.

Crook took a little note from his pocket. "That," he said, "was lot 87 star then, with no name. I had no idea the steward was a buyer. That accounts for four magnums altogether, including the one we drank. If you *have* the lucky bottle, Mr. Merrick, the sooner we see it the better; the sooner the better, in fact, in any case. But there's the inquest, and they want me here.

Which brings me back to my story. I was visiting your old friend Mr. Clifton on this very matter of the Tokay. He had a magnum himself."

"What? No! You don't say!"

"Yes I do. And more—he bought it himself at the sale, so that you and he must have been in the room together here at Lawson's, four days ago—rubbed shoulders, as likely as not!"

Lyman W. Merrick rose and tramped agitatedly about the room.

"I've reckoned myself a hustler," he said as he went, with his fingers in the hair over each of his ears—"I've reckoned myself a hustler most o' my life, and I've been called a hustler by them that can hustle a few on their own; but these hustlings are getting a shade too jumpy for me. Getting older, I s'pose. What I've seen and heard since I opened that paper at breakfast this morning is enough to hustle the senses out of any man's head, and I'm not sure whether I've got any of 'em or not now. I say," he added, turning suddenly to Crook, "I s'pose I really *am* awake? Do you 'low I'm quite awake, Mr. Crook?"

"Quite awake, Mr. Merrick," Crook answered with

a smile, "and waiting to hear about my last night's adventure, I've no doubt."

Merrick sat down, and Crook told his story in detail. He produced Mr. Clifton's letter inviting him to Downs Lodge to exhibit the old Chinese kakemono; he told of how he had learned Mr. Clifton's name and address from Symons, the auctioneer's clerk; he described the curious house and his more curious reception; and last, dropping his voice with something of a furtive look towards Daisy Merrick, he described the disappearance of his false host, and his ghastly discoveries in kitchen and library.

Merrick rose again, and walked about as he had done before.

"Poor old fellow," he said, with genuine distress in his voice; "poor old man. A splendid old gentleman like him—for he *was* splendid, up an' down, though I only saw him once, barrin' the other day, when I may have seen him or not, but didn't know. To be cut an' killed like that, after all, in his own chair, an' me as near as I was, an' not near enough to stop it! Mr. Crook, it's—it's—" the words came rather like sobs—"it's pretty tough, I 'low!"

"And then—then they arrested *you,* Mr. Crook?" Daisy asked.

"Yes—and a very natural thing for them to do. There was I, a stranger, in the house, the housemaid out, and the master and the housekeeper both murdered. But it didn't last long, of course. They brought me back here before midnight, and now they're out all over the country after Pritchard—the man who really is guilty, without much doubt, I should say." And Crook went on to tell what he had heard of the history of the fugitive.

"Poor old friend!" mused Merrick, once again, sitting now with his hands on his knees. "Helping a man over a snag again, too—just like him! Helping somebody again, and this is what he got for it! Cut his throat for three hundred dollars in the safe! Come!" he added more briskly, jumping to his feet, "this ain't no sort of a way for a live man to hoe this row! Sittin' and grievin' is no way to catch Mr. Pritchard. And it's him that's to be caught, and will be, if my bottom dollar will catch him! Can't we see the police?"

"Of course we can. But the inquest is this afternoon—quite soon, in fact. The coroner seems to be what you would call a hustler, and apparently his work is a little slack just now. But have you lunched? There is barely time."

IV.

THE inquests were held in the hall of Downs Lodge, the bodies having been removed to the coach-house. As many of the public as could squeeze into the hall were there, and the front steps and forepart of the grounds were crowded. Mr. Merrick and his daughter were given favoured places in the hall on the representations of Harvey Crook, and proceedings were begun with exact punctuality, the business-like coroner using a combined procedure which enabled the two inquiries to be conducted with as little repetition of form and evidence as possible.

The police gave evidence of having been called to the spot, and of what they found when they got there. The divisional surgeon described the condition of the bodies and the positions in which they had been found, and stated his scientific opinion on the causes of death in each case—opinions given purely formally, of course, since it was plain to everybody that no man could live with his throat cut as Mr. Clifton's had been, nor anybody, man or woman, with such injuries to the head as the housekeeper had suffered.

But, of course, the chief witness was Harvey Crook. He produced the letter of invitation which he had received from Mr. Clifton, his own reply to which, as well as his own first letter, was in the hands of the police. He told of his reception at the house, and described, as closely as possible, the person of the man who had entertained him, and whom he had supposed to be Mr. Clifton. In short, he retold, with more particular detail, the story Merrick and Daisy had already heard. This in every particular but one. For, of course, he said nothing of the Tokay, beyond the simple fact, which was all that was needed, that the man who had entertained him had brought in cold food and a bottle of wine. He had come to exhibit his old Chinese painting, and the wine, Tokay or other, was no business for this jury—or, at any rate, so it seemed to Crook at the time.

Then there was the evidence of the housemaid——largely a description of the missing Mr. James

Pritchard, tallying exactly with the description of his host already given by Crook; how long Pritchard had been at the house, what he had done, and so forth. The evidence, also, of Mr. Clifton's solicitor, who knew something of Pritchard's earlier career, and had letters and other papers in the matter. And in the end the jury gave their verdicts, as everybody knew they must: in each case it was "Wilful murder by James Pritchard."

Now, although Crook had a general reason of prudence for not mentioning the matter of the Tokay in his evidence, and no reason at all for mentioning it, he had, in addition, one very particular and immediate reason for acting as he did. For, as he began his testimony, his eyes wandered toward the door, and there, behind the rest of the people who had found standing room, was Hahn, eyes and ears wide open, noting every word. And when his examination was over, and Crook was at liberty to move about as he pleased, Hahn was gone.

Now here was a point in the game for Hahn. For though there might have been nothing suspicious in Crook's visit to Mr. Clifton as he had told it, and as, in fact, it had occurred, there remained the simple fact that he had returned to Southampton from London quicker than Hahn could get there, and it was from a Southampton hotel that his letters to Mr. Clifton were dated. That was quite enough for a man like Hahn. He knew that he was not alone in his search for the Green Eye of Goona—had perhaps even begun to suspect the inner meaning of his reception in Mr. Norie's studio.

So the crowd broke up, and Lyman W. Merrick, in company with Crook, sought the chief constable, eager to do what might be done to bring the murderer to justice. Crook explained in a few words the relation in which Merrick stood to the murdered man, and Merrick opened business straight away.

"See here, Mr. Chief Constable," he said, "I want to offer a reward for the apprehension of this fellow. There's nothing against that, is there?"

No, it seemed there was no particular law against it. The police no longer offered rewards themselves, but there was nothing to prevent a private person doing so.

"Very good, sir. Then I will give five thousand dollars—one thousand pounds, that is—to the man who arrests the murderer of Mr. Basil Clifton. Is five thousand enough? If not, don't mind telling me. I can double it."

"Quite enough—plenty," answered the chief constable. "Even too much, I think I should say."

"Then that's a good fault, sir, and we'll let it stand. And beyond that I'll give more. I'll give one thousand dollars to any other man whom you think deserves it for his work on the case—one man or more, just as many as you tell me. And now, if it's no way against the rules, I'd like to take a look over the house with my friend Mr. Harvey Crook, to see just how it all happened."

There was no difficulty about that, especially as the more unpleasant traces of the tragedies had been now removed by the police.

"Everything else has been left as it was," said the chief constable, "and, of course, if either of you gentlemen sees anything suggestive or interesting, in view of your own knowledge of the poor old gentleman, and of the circumstances, I hope you'll mention it."

They went first to the dining-room, where the table lay just as Crook had left it, and the guttered candles were hanging over the silver candlesticks. There lay the remains of the dinner, and on the sideboard stood the two decanters of Tokay, with the empty magnum by their side.

"Here is the magnum you sold," said Crook, turning to Merrick. "It was opened especially for me—or rather, I opened it myself. Mr. Merrick sold some bottles of Tokay by auction when he arrived in England," Crook explained to the chief constable, "and Mr. Clifton bought one, without knowing who the seller was."

The chief constable nodded pleasantly, as though the matter were a very interesting one for the parties concerned, but of no particular moment to him; and Mr. Merrick lifted the empty magnum, tilted it and shook it. But Crook had already told him that this magnum had been drawn a blank, and he acted in mere curiosity.

Crook led the way along the corridor and down the stairs, repeating as he went the story of his questing and calling for his host in the dark stillness of last night. The kitchen door stood wide open now, but the floor was still wet from the recent scrubbing that had been so necessary.

"He must have stepped over the woman's body here," exclaimed the chief constable, "each time he came downstairs for plates or what not for the dinner he gave you, Mr. Crook." And Daisy, clinging tight to her father's arm, shuddered at the thought.

They came up from the lower floor, and as they gained the landing Merrick chanced to glance up the staircase, and saw a flat glass case hanging on the wall at the next landing.

"Why," he exclaimed, "look there! If there ain't my old wampum!"

They climbed the intervening flight of stairs, and there the wampum hung, sure enough, displayed to advantage against the wall behind the glass. Tears stood in Merrick's eyes as he gazed at it. "There it is, Daisy," he repeated, in a curious sort of half-pleased voice. "There it is. That's it!"

"It's the only thing I ever gave him," he went on again, after a pause; "and it don't seem much for what he did for me, and trusting me, too, a stranger. But I'm mighty pleased to see he took care of it—mighty pleased to see that, I am. Yes; it's a comfort, now, to see he thought something of it—perhaps more than I

10*

did. You'd say, gentlemen, looking at that glass case and all that, he did think something of it, wouldn't you?"

"Oh, of course," answered Crook. "Didn't you see the numberless valuable things lying about below loose? And then, look at this glass case!"

"Ah," the American answered, "I'm mighty glad to see that case, and to know you think he thought something of that wampum. It's sort of lifted a load off my mind, gentlemen, in a foolish sort o' way."

And now they turned to the library where Merrick's old friend had met his death. Just as when Crook had first seen it the night before, there lay books and books everywhere, high and low. But now the blood-stains were gone, and the poor torn body had been carried away from the chair in which Crook had found it. The door of the little safe still stood open, the little sheet-iron drawers were still tumbled on the floor, and the drawers of the writing-table were splintered and gaping just as they had been left; and the chief constable explained the meaning of all these things as he pointed them out.

"Nothing else seems to have been touched," he concluded, casually pushing open the cupboard under an old glazed bookcase. "Here you are, everything seems in order; and there's a bottle of wine like the other." .

And in truth there was; for there before their eyes stood another magnum of Tokay, the fellow to the one that Crook had opened the night before, and one of the dozen without a possible doubt!

"But," said Merrick,—"but—he only bought one?"

"Yes," Crook replied, "that is certain. I have it from the auctioneer's clerk that he only bought one. That is certain."

"Had another already, I expect," observed the chief constable carelessly.

Crook lifted the great bottle and saw that the cork had been drawn; also some of the wine was gone—three or four glasses, perhaps. He took the magnum to the light of the window, held the cork fast, and slowly tilted it. Nothing was there—nothing but the wine. No diamond came tumbling from the bottom into the neck.

Merrick and Crook looked one at the other, and put the bottle back. What did it mean? The bottle had been opened, certainly.

They made toward the door, and the chief constable marched into the corridor. Merrick turned to Crook and whispered.

"What does it mean?" he said. "That scoundrel knew what was in the house, and yet he opened a new magnum for you! Why? How did this one get here? *Was* it only for sixty or seventy pounds that he did murder—or was it for something more? Something in that bottle of wine?"

The two men looked each in the other's face and passed out in the wake of the chief constable.

———————

V.

MR. POOLEY'S MAGNUM.

I.

"I GUESS this little holiday of ours is likely to be a hustlin'er sort of holiday than we allowed," observed Mr. Lyman W. Merrick. "And we *did* allow to hustle some, too."

Harvey Crook smiled. He remembered the sanguine programme arranged by his American friend and his daughter on board the *Rajapur,* with its two thousand square miles or so of Great Britain per diem. Daisy Merrick smiled, too; which was a pleasant thing in itself, and interesting to any person who might have been noticing the fact that she and Crook were getting into a habit of smiling together.

"However," Mr. Merrick pursued, "there's to be no holiday-making till we've introduced ourselves to Mr. Pritchard, and I'll see that man arrested if I have to stay in England the rest of my life. You and I'll see about that, Mr. Crook."

"Anything I can do, of course, I will," Crook said. "But I doubt if either of us can do as much as the police, who are organised specially for such work. Moreover"—Crook smiled again—"I have a little hunt of my own in progress, as you know, Mr. Merrick. There's that green diamond! That to me is very much what your five hundred dollars' worth of land was twenty-six years ago. Though of course I don't expect so much out of this as you have derived from your own little speculation!"

"Yes, yes—the green diamond," Mr. Merrick answered thoughtfully. "There's such a deal of excitement about to-day that I was clean forgetting that; though it isn't the sort of thing you'd think one would forget easily, either. Well, what's your next move with that?"

They had returned to the hotel after the inquest, and were refreshing themselves with tea. It was a little late for tea, but the inquest was responsible for that, and it still lacked some hour or two to dinner-time.

"My next move," said Crook slowly, "I can't pretend to prophesy. Except, of course, that I want to examine—or want you to examine—that bottle of Tokay you have in London."

"Of course—that's the first thing. Why, I have had such a day—finding Mr. Clifton, and finding him dead, and getting hustled up and down this way and that, that I positively began to forget buying that bottle of McNab. Snakes! What a piece of luck if the diamond should be in that!"

"Well," Crook responded, "it's an eight-to-one-chance against, of course—which otherwise mathematically expressed, is a chance of one in nine. There were a dozen magnums to begin with, and it's certain that the diamond was in one of them. The first we opened and drank on the *Rajapur*. It wasn't in that. The second got to Mr. Norie the artist—it certainly wasn't in that, since I poured every drop from it myself. Then there was the magnum that poor Mr. Clifton bought—the one brought me in the course of that amazing dinner last night. As to that I can certify also—I decanted it myself. That leaves nine of the dozen unaccounted for, and one of those is the mysterious bottle we ourselves discovered this afternoon, opened, in Mr. Clifton's bookcase—a very mysterious bottle that."

"Mysterious it is." Mr. Merrick slapped his knee and nodded vehemently. "Mysterious it is, I say, and it may supply a, bigger motive for those murders than the few hundred dollars that are gone."

"Quite likely," Crook responded, "but the solution of that mystery must wait till the murderer is caught— even if we reach it then. Meantime, we mustn't neglect the other magnums, for after all we have nothing but the wildest conjecture as to this. I must waste no time, for the very magnum containing that great green diamond may be being uncorked at this very moment! I must waste no time, as I say, and yet for the life of me I can't see how next to employ it, or where to look now. At any rate, we'll have a look at *your* bottle as soon as we are in London again. Meantime, I might go and see the auctioneer's clerk again; though if he had anything to tell me he would have been round here with it."

"It was he who gave you the names of some of the buyers, wasn't it?" Daisy asked.

"Yes, as far as he could. Though that wasn't very far, as I have told you."

"Well, now, Mr. Crook," Daisy said, with a whimsical smile, "I wonder it has never occurred to you to ask anybody else who was present at the sale, besides the auctioneer's clerk—me, for instance!"

"You! Why, of course—if you can remember——"

"Yes"—Daisy laughed—"I *can* remember more than father can, anyway, I'm sure! I don't remember much that can be of use perhaps, but I do remember that two of the passengers on the *Rajapur* bought magnums—two passengers at least. There were Mr. Pooley and Mr. Allen."

"I knew Allen bought one," Crook observed. "He gave his name, and the clerk had it down on the marked catalogue. Come—we'll try for Allen next. I should be able to get at him somehow through the steamship office, no doubt. But who was Pooley?"

"Oh, I expect you wouldn't have heard his name. He was a very quiet passenger, and we only knew it through an accident. A box of his was put into father's cabin by mistake, and he came round with the steward after it. He was a clean-shaven, rather overdressed man, but quiet in his ways, and he kept very much in his own quarters. Perhaps you don't remember him?"

"I don't think I do."

"Well, at any rate, he bought one of the magnums. Let me recollect, now. When the first lot was put up there was a long pause—nobody seemed to want the wine, or to know what to bid. It began low, and McNab, the steward, got the magnum for nine shillings. Father remembers that—the price startled him, I tell you!"

"It did!" Mr. Merrick assented.

"A funny little man bought the next lot—a very carefully brushed and oiled little man, with very loud clothes. He bought four magnums one after another for ten shillings each, and gave the name of Smith. He was a wine-merchant's traveller, they said. And then Mr. Allen bought a bottle, and then Mr. Pooley."

Crook was consulting the copy he had made of this part of Symons's marked catalogue. "Yes," he said, "and then a bottle was sold to the artist, Mr. Norie. The next was number ninety-five star, and the name Curtice is against that. But stay—there *is* something I

can do now—before dinner, even. The shipping office is in London, but the ship must still be here. I'll go and knock up McNab, the steward."

The *Rajapur* carried cargo of a superior kind, as well as passengers, and was still discharging pending repairs. McNab, the chief steward, might have obtained leave to come to London by rail, leaving his assistant in charge, since the passengers had all left the ship. But the thought of such an extravagance would have appalled his thrifty mind. By sticking to his post as long as possible, he not only saved his railway fare, but also lived at the expense of his employers; and nothing short of an obvious pecuniary balance on the other side could have induced him to forego such advantages. So that Crook reached the steward's pantry of the *Rajapur* to find McNab still in it.

McNab, dour and distrustful, waited while Crook explained that he was anxious to find the addresses of Mr. Allen and Mr. Pooley, late passengers on the *Rajapur*, and would be glad of any help to that end. Then the steward cleared his throat and said: "Ha, hum. Ye'll ken it's nae pairt o' my duties to gie addresses, or assist in gettin' addresses, o' passengers that hae left the ship an' are no any further concern of mine?"

"Oh yes, of course. If you are able to give me any help, of course I shall be very grateful"—here McNab looked sourer than ever—"and, of course, I'll pay whatever you think is right for your trouble."

At this the McNab no longer looked sour, but rather disappointed. "Oh aye," he said, "that's weel enough, but I'm thinkin' I can do naething for ye. I ken nae mair o' their addresses than ye ken yersel'! But I'll remember what ye say, if ye'll let me hae your ain address."

"Certainly. Though I wanted the information without delay."

McNab shook his head. Then he said, looking curiously in Crook's face, "There's a curious thing about they names, Mr. Crook. Mr. Allen and Mr. Pooley each bought one o' they muckle big bottles o' Tokay at the sale—the same that ye sold Mr. Merrick; an' I bought one myself!"

"Well?"

"Weel, Mr. Merrick bought mine back frae me. Now you come yersel' and want the addresses of twa ither buyers; and I've had ither inquiries. I suspeecion I've sold Mr. Merrick that bottle too cheap!"

Plainly the shrewd McNab smelt a rat somewhere.

"Indeed!" Crook observed carelessly. "And as to the other inquiries, I expect some of them came from a man named Hahn, didn't they? A man of near about fifty, not so tall as me, with a short, grey beard. Speaks excellent English, but is a foreigner?"

"Weel, Mr. Crook, I won't deny but what you seem to ken him. And I've guid reason to believe I could have done better with my bottle with him than with Mr. Merrick. But it's no' him alone has been makin' inquiries."

"Who else?"

"The police! Aye, the police have been here for Mr. Pooley's address!"

"The police!"

"Aye, the police. I couldna tell them more than I could tell you, o' course, and equally o' course they told me naethin', and for why they came I ken naethin'. But it was the police, an' a plain-clothes policeman at that!"

So with this information—and it was surprising

enough—Harvey Crook was fain to return to his dinner. The steward watched him as he left the ship, and returned to his pantry with many wise shakes of the head. Plainly, Mr. McNab was convinced that big things were afoot; and even though he had not a ghost of a notion what the big things were, he was resolved to squeeze a profit from them if any profit were to be squeezed.

II.

To Harvey Crook the puzzle before him became multiplied by a hundred. What did this mean—the police? Was it possible that Hahn and his tricks had been betrayed, and that the police were in as eager search of those dispersed magnums of Tokay as he himself was? In that case he felt he might as well give up the chase on his own account and turn to more profitable business. The police, with all their elaborate machinery, their armies of trained detectives, their command of every source of information, could do more in an hour than he could attempt in a week. But the true explanation of the matter came in a very little while.

Crook made no delay on his way from the dock, but went straight back to the hotel. True, he would be too early for dinner, but why not just as well wait in the company of Mr. Merrick and Daisy—for it would be futile to pretend that she had nothing to do with the matter—as not?"

He found his friends in their private sitting-room with visitors. One visitor was a youngish-looking man, clean-shaven, broad-framed but bony, who looked rather like a prize-fighter a little over-trained, and with an exceptionally intelligent head; the other was the chief constable who had accompanied them over Mr. Clifton's house only an hour or two ago.

"Here's my friend Mr. Crook," Merrick said as Crook entered. "Though I doubt if he can tell you more than we can. This gentleman," he said, turning to Crook, "is a detective of the London force, Sergeant Wickes. It seems we've been travelling in bad company. That Mr. Pooley, the quiet passenger in the loud clothes, is wanted by the police!"

"Well—the police would like to know where he is

—that's all," the chief constable said. "He's a notorious character, you see, and one of the sort the police *must* keep track of if they can, you know, or they'll be in serious mischief and away again before they can be stopped. The Scotland Yard authorities lost track of him some little while back, and only just received information that he had been to the great Durbar in India. He is a great swell in his way, you see, and that is just the sort of place he'd go to, and make it pay him, somehow, too. It is discovered now that he returned in the *Rajapur* and landed a few days back, with you; but where he's gone they can't tell, and that is what the sergeant here is trying to find out. He has been to the ship, and he has seen the passenger-list, but that tells nothing. He came to the Southampton police also, of course, and I, knowing that you came over in the same boat, brought him here. I'm sure you'll tell him anything you may have noticed on the voyage."

"I would willingly, of course," Crook replied, "but really, I noticed nothing."

"Never spoke to him, I suppose?" the detective asked keenly.

"Never."

"This lady and gentleman here tell me that he had very little luggage, kept very much to himself during the voyage, and they saw nothing of him after he landed except that he went into a local auction room and bought some wine. Is there anything you can remember to add to that, sir?"

"No," Crook replied; "nothing whatever."

"Thank you," replied Wickes, rising promptly. "Sorry to trouble you, of course, but police duty's very necessary, as you will understand. I must make inquiries in other directions. Buying wine would look rather like staying in Southampton, at least for a bit, but it's pretty certain he isn't here. Gone to London in all probability. Good evening!"

When their visitors had gone Mr. Merrick looked across at Crook and clicked his tongue suggestively.

"What does that mean?" he observed. "Not the police inquiries, of course—they're natural enough, I guess—but why does a dead sharp like that, a well-known tough of the highest circles in scoundrelism, anxious to come into the country without attracting notice from the police—why does that sort of man stop to buy himself a magnum of Tokay? A big hefty lump of a bottle to lug around, too, for a man with nothing else but a portmanteau of clothes, and anxious to dance around flying light. It seems to me that a tough like that don't buy the bottle for the sake of the wine, anyway?"

It was certainly very suggestive, and Crook said so.

"Is it possible," he added, "that he could have known of Hahn's little game, and cut into it by buying the bottle containing the jewel? It might almost seem like it at first. But did you hear any more about this fellow Pooley? Anything before I came in, I mean?"

"Oh yes—in a general sort of way. The detective wasn't tellin' much about him, but the chief constable 'lowed he was a rare tough in the heavy swindle way, with miscellaneous abilities. A big bill forgery, a bank robbery, or a gamble with stocked cards—they are all very much in his line, it seems, if the boodle's big enough. He isn't above bunco-steering if the plunder's likely to be large. He's strictly honest, they 'low, in any matter that there's not much to be made out of, and he only condescends to touch big things. Now, just you think of this. Ain't it mighty likely he's in this diamond ramp, and came over in the same steamer to keep an eye on you, while you, all innocent, took the risk of bringing the plunder over? Now, don't that strike you as a pretty probable guess? And if that's so, that green diamond was in that magnum that Mr. Pooley bought and walked off with!"

Crook was thoughtful for a few moments before replying. Then he said, "No, I don't agree. It looks right enough at first sight, but not after. For how should he know which particular magnum that diamond was concealed in? Hahn himself doesn't know, plainly. He is dancing about distractedly trying to get hold of any of the bottles he can, and enduring all sorts of trouble in the search. Plainly, he depended on getting the case intact and so finding the jewel where he left it with no trouble. And even if he knew, and if Pooley knew, in what part of the case the bottle stood which contained the stone, how should he know the bottle when it was one among eleven, put up one after another at a sale? He didn't bid for any other bottles, did he?"

Daisy Merrick shook her head. "I don't think he did," she said. "At any rate, that is the only one he bought."

"Just so; and if it was impossible that he could know which of those bottles held the diamond, the assumption is that he didn't know that a diamond was in any one of them, else he would have bought the lot— or tried to buy them, at any rate. And if that is so, why did he buy the one?"

But that was a conundrum that nobody could answer. After a few random speculations, Mr. Merrick wound up with this dictum: "Guessin's and wonderin's won't hoe this row. There's a great diamond in one of a few bottles of wine, and a dead sharp, with a natural instinct for plunder, has gone off with one of those bottles. That's enough. Mr. Pooley's the victim to go for next!"

"Well, yes," Crook assented with a smile, "unless we find the stone in *your* magnum! But what I'm mostly concerned about now is where to go for Mr. Pooley!"

With this the waiter began to lay the cloth for dinner, and there was silence, save for the little noise the waiter made at his work. Crook sat deep in thought, gazing into the fire. Presently he stood up and spoke.

"Waiter," he said, "you have the London papers

here, I know. Can you get me those London papers
for the last three days or so? I suppose they'll be kept
somewhere?"

"Well, sir; no, sir; not kept, sir; not very long, I
should say, sir," the man answered. "I don't quite
know what 'ud become of 'em, sir, but I'll inquire, if
you like."

"Very well," Crook answered. "If you can bring
me all your London papers for the past three days,
and bring them in half an hour, I'll give you five
shillings."

At this the waiter started off with a bounce, and
there was danger of delay in the dinner preparations.
The papers came, however, and as the preparations for
the meal were completed, Crook examined their advertisement columns carefully, comparing one with another,
returning to a paper already examined, and then comparing again. At length he selected one paper from
the bunch, kicked the others aside, and sent the waiter
for a London Directory. A single reference to this
mighty tome satisfied him, and he rose, ready for
dinner.

"I shall make a shot in the dark," he said, "or

pretty nearly in the dark, seeing that there's no other course left open. Wish me luck! That's my selection."

He pointed to an advertisement nearly at the top of the "agony" column of the *Standard* of the day before, and Merrick, greatly mystified, read this:—

ZAG.—Come back here again, either at one thirty or eight o'clock. MELDON.

"That your selection?" repeated Merrick doubtfully. "Well, you might tell me of twenty such selections without excitin' me any. What does it mean?"

"I won't be sure, but it may mean one thing, and that's my shot. It *may* mean an address, and that address *may* be Pooley's!"

Mr. Merrick shook his head. "I give that up," he said.

They sat to dinner, and Crook explained in fragmentary bursts, at such times as the waiter was out of the room. The explanation, pieced together, being to this effect:—

"Any attempt to get at this fellow Pooley must begin with some sort of a guess as to what he would do first on landing quietly in England, as he has done. Now, such a fellow, of course, always works with con-federates—the sort of crime he lives on is committed by accomplished gangs, invariably. Consequently, it strikes me that the first thing he would do would be to put himself in communication with his friends. How? Naturally, you would say, by letter; and if that is what he has done, I am off the track, and I don't see what to do. But there would almost certainly be objections to communication by letter. That sort of person doesn't stay longer in one place than he can help, for obvious reasons. Pooley has been out of the country for some time, and any attempt to communicate with his 'pals' by post would probably lead to a miscarriage of the letter, the falling of that letter into dangerous hands, and all sorts of complication. What other expedient is open to him? Obviously one—and one notoriously known to be used for the communications of persons of this kind—the 'agony' columns of the newspapers. I'm not sure it wasn't your own advertisement that turned my mind in that direction. At any rate, I resolved to look at the London papers of the last few days and examine any suspicious-looking advertisement. Well, here is one—the only really suspicious one I can see."

Mr. Merrick took another look at it.

"I don't seem to suspicion it yet," he remarked.

"Doesn't it look a little redundant? These advertisements are paid for according to the number of words, I believe, and that is why they are usually expressed in the briefest possible language. Very good. Then why not say, 'Come back at one thirty or eight?' That would be quite enough if the message meant what it seems to mean. 'Here,' 'again,' 'either,' and 'o'clock' are redundant. That is the first peculiarity that struck me. Then I saw another. Now read every other word of that advertisement, beginning with 'Zag' and skipping the alternate words. Then you get this message: 'Zag. —Back again at thirty-eight, Meldon.' Now isn't that *very* suspicious? Meldon, of course, might be an assumed name, but it isn't likely. If it were a *new* assumed name the confederate would fail to recognise it, and if it were an old one the police would spot it; and in any case it would be unnecessary, for it is plain that 'Zag' in the beginning must be the identification word, by which the gang recognise their communications. Why shouldn't it mean an address? Thirty-eight, Meldon Street, or Road, or what not? And here, sure enough, is a Meldon Street in the London Directory, and all alone. No Meldon Square, or Road, or anything but this one Meldon Street. It is near Euston, you see, and there *is* a thirty-eight in the street (though the particular house is not entered here), for you will perceive that the 'Bell' public-house is No. 40!"

Mr. Merrick's eyes began to sparkle.

"This gets positively interesting!" he said. "Here's an adventure, or something mighty like it. Clear enough *somebody* has 'come back' and taken lodgings in London, and somebody who wishes to keep pretty close and secret; and the police sagaciate that Pooley must ha' gone straight to London after buyin' that magnum of wine. It's a chance, and I allow it's an adventure! Mr. Crook, I feel young again—I do! I haven't had an adventure—not properly to be called an adventure—for twenty-five years. I'm on this one if you'll let me in. Come, Daisy, d'you think you're equal to runnin' up to London again to-night? Isn't there a train?"

"Yes," Crook answered; "the last goes at nine-thirty."

"Then we're on the nine-thirty to London, aren't we, Daisy? I want to take a look at that bottle of my own, and we'll do that to-night. And to-morrow we'll investigate the architectural attractions of that venerable pile, thirty-eight, Meldon Street, near Euston Station, London! That is, Mr. Crook, if that's your plan, and if I'm not intermeddlin'?"

"Not at all. I'm delighted to have a friend at hand, of course. But you mustn't be disappointed if we draw a dead blank. As I said, it's something of a shot in the dark, though there should be something like a fair chance for us."

III.

MR. MERRICK'S magnum of Tokay, late the property of McNab, being carefully unswathed that night from the middle of the clothes in a portmanteau, was found to be—just a magnum of Tokay and nothing else. It was not necessary to open the bottle. Carefully wiped clean with a towel and held against a strong electric light, the Eye of Goona, if it had been there, would have been detected by the keen eyes in search of it, even though it might have escaped the vision of a person not in the secret. Tilted on end, no jewel came rolling toward the thinner neck—nothing. The great green diamond was still to be found.

But Mr. Merrick seemed rather pleased at his failure than otherwise, since it gave zest to the adventure he promised himself. It seemed that he would have been almost disappointed to find the jewel in his own bottle.

"Nothing there," he said. "No! That dead sharp Pooley didn't buy that other magnum to play skittles with, you bet! No, sir! He's a mile deeper than we guess, and a fathom or two under that! Thirty-eight, Meldon Street, near Euston, to-morrow morning!"

"Very well, we'll be there."

"And disguised! Disguised, my boy! No good two passengers fresh from the *Rajapur*—and us especially, seeing it's the Tokay biz—no good us goin' cavortin' around after Mr. Pooley in biled shirts an' new store clothes! Ge-whiz! I'll have red whiskers!"

"I think we'd better avoid the whiskers," Crook observed. "We should be some time getting them, and

they are apt to come off at the wrong moment. No—
we'd better waste no time disguising. We'll wear in-
conspicuous things—tweeds or the like. I've an idea
that people unused to disguises are apt to fail to play
up to them and so attract attention. I think we must
leave that alone."

Mr. Merrick assented on his better judgment, though
with regret. Plainly he was feeling young again,
and a disguise would have been an addition to the fun.

The morning found the two early afoot and strolling
along Portland Place, and so, by Park Crescent, to the
Euston Road. Merrick would have had a cab, such
was his elderly impetuosity, but the more cautious Crook
dissuaded him.

"No good getting there too soon," he said. "I
expect it's the sort of street where strangers, so very
early in the day, might be noticed; and a cab would
cause a particular stir. A little walk will do us
good."

So they walked, and with no haste. They passed
the Hampstead Road, took a turning to the left, and
then another; and so came to Meldon Street.

It was a decent enough street of its sort—not

exactly dirty, and not exactly Belgravian. The houses had areas and front steps, and in more than one window a card with the word "Apartments" was displayed. They soon perceived that No. 38 must be on the left hand at the far end, and that it was probably the very last house before the "Bell," the public-house to which the Post Office Directory had already introduced Crook.

"I think we should stroll casually past and turn into the pub," Crook suggested.

No. 38 offered no information on its face. Dusty curtains, a chair-back visible through the first-floor window, more dusty curtains below, in the area-window, and that was all. Next door the "Bell" stood; and it was a tavern with a yard-entry at its side, and, indeed, under some part of its upper floors. One entrance to the bar was in this yard-entry, and it was clear that the yard led back into an adjoining street. Into the yard they turned, and looked about them.

"Best to learn the ground first," observed Crook; and as the words left his lips Merrick snatched at his shoulder and pulled him back into the archway from which they were emerging.

"There he is!" he exclaimed, in an excited whisper. "On him! We're on him!"

Crook had been looking straight ahead down the yard, but Merrick had turned his head as they emerged from under the shadow of the passage.

"He's at the window, shaving," he said. "Be careful how you show, and you'll see him."

Crook advanced with great care and peeped. Sure enough, at the first-floor window of the next-door house a man was shaving at a glass suspended on the window frame, and as he removed his hand to wipe his razor Crook saw his late fellow-passenger Pooley.

"He hasn't seen us," Crook said; "he was intent on his work. See here, now. If that is a billiard-room on the first floor of this place, we are going to play at billiards. We should be able to see in at that window."

The room Crook spoke of stood out at a right angle from the hinder face of the public-house building. They entered the side door of the house, ordered drinks, and discovered that though there was no billiard-table in the room in question, there was a bagatelle-board. In the circumstances billiards and bagatelle were all one to them; so they carried their drinks upstairs. The boy who would have otherwise attended them was busy with pots, and as it was impossible for the visitors to leave the floor above without coming under the eye of the landlord, they were allowed to have the room to themselves.

And so they sat down to a spell of wearisome and seemingly aimless watching that told sadly on Merrick's patience. Pooley soon left the window and carried his mirror with him, and for some little while they saw nothing of him. The suspicion began to grow upon them that Pooley must have left the house, when suddenly, as they crouched, one at each side of the window, watching, they were amazed to see placed on the table that stood before the window an unmistakable big bottle. It was the magnum of Tokay, with the cork drawn!

And now they became aware that Pooley had a visitor. For the bottle was taken up and set down again once or twice, and by different hands. And at length two heads and their pairs of shoulders bent suddenly before the window. Clearly Pooley and his visitor were intently examining some small object.

What it was they could not see, though Merrick strained his neck a dozen ways in the attempt. The visitor's back was turned to the near side of the window, and shut out all possible view of the centre of interest. So the two remained for some little while, and then withdrew from the window as suddenly as they had appeared at it, leaving the bottle standing on the table.

There was a pause of a few minutes, and then Pooley, now wearing a hat, appeared again at the table, and began, with great care, to re-cork the magnum.

"A fresh cork," Crook observed. "I expect the other crumbled."

The cork driven well home, Pooley produced sealing-wax and a candle, and soon had covered the cork with a broken smear that might well have passed for an old seal. Then he lifted a hand-bag from under the table, put the bottle in it, and instantly whisked the bag off into the obscurity of the room.

"Enough, I think," said Crook. "They're going

out with it, I believe. Our game of bagatelle is finished."

They descended to the bar, and while Crook settled with the landlord Merrick watched from the entry.

"They're off," he repeated excitedly, as Crook joined him. "There they go!" And Crook could see that Pooley and his visitor were already half-way down the street, Pooley carrying the bag.

Then came an exciting chase through the streets leading to Euston Road. Crook held Merrick back till the pair ahead had turned the first corner, and then a run was necessary in order to get a view of them before they took a fresh turn. In the Euston Road Pooley called a cab; and here, in this great busy thoroughfare, it was easy enough to follow in another without attracting the notice of the enemy.

The cab ahead made for Tottenham Court Road, and turned south through that thoroughfare, with the cab behind in close chase.

"We're on it!" cried Merrick exultingly, "—or on something, anyway!"

"Something, certainly," Crook answered thoughtfully. "But what it is I can't guess. I'm not sure,

12*

even though the magnum of Tokay is in it, why we
are following that cab, except that it seems the only
thing we can do just now."

Along Tottenham Court Road, across Oxford Street,
and down Charing Cross Road the leading hansom
went, with its follower never far away.   Indeed, a short
block of traffic by the Palace Theatre brought the two
into touching distance, and so they went the rest of the
way.

Across Trafalgar Square the route lay to the part
of Charing Cross by Whitehall, and there, scarcely
beyond the corner, the cab ahead swung into a narrow
turning and pulled up.   Crook's cabman was plainly
a man of ready resource, for he refrained from following further than the mouth of the alley, across which
he drew up his cab.

"This'll be best, sir, won't it?" asked the cabman,
through the roof-trap.

"Quite right," Crook answered.   "You shall have
an extra shilling for that.   Wait a moment."

Through the near-side window of the hansom they
saw Pooley and his companion alight, pay their cabman, and enter a door.

"Come, we're after them!" cried Crook, springing from the cab, and thrusting a half-crown into the driver's hand.

They hurried along the passage, and saw that the building into which the chase had disappeared was a new one—the newest in the row; and a glance was enough to show that half the offices it contained were still unlet. A lift-cage stood before the door, but apparently there was nobody to work it, and up the stone staircase footsteps could be heard. A glance up the well showed that Pooley and his companion were ascending, a flight or two up. Merrick and Crook followed, getting as near as they dared without exhibiting themselves.

The men ahead went on, flight after flight, to the very top landing. Then there was a knock, a door opened, and after a few indistinct words it was closed again. A cautious approach showed that the door bore the words, "Isaacs, Agent," and nothing more.

All remained quiet within. Crook and Merrick looked this way and that, but this building offered no friendly observation point.

"Well," said Crook, "here we are, and what have

we gained by coming? There is the bottle of wine we are after, behind that door, after having been opened and corked again at Meldon Street."

"The name is Isaacs," observed Merrick. "The sort of name you might expect at a place where they would come to sell a big diamond, I guess?"

"But why the bottle? And so carefully re-sealed? Besides, a man like Pooley wouldn't come here to sell such a stone as the Eye of Goona. He'd take it to the Continent—to Amsterdam. He could deal more freely there, and get a better price. No, I don't understand this move at all. There is an empty office just below—under Isaacs's. If we are to wait, we may as well wait there, where we can get out of sight if necessary."

They went to the room Crook had indicated, and waited. There was no sound from above; they waited and still they waited, and ere long waiting grew tiresome.

"Come," said Crook at last, "I want my lunch, and I vote we put an end to this. The police want Pooley, and we have found him. New Scotland Yard is close by, and——"

From the room above came a long-drawn human sound that was neither a sigh, nor a sob, nor a shriek, but which had something of the character of each. Then silence. Then a loud burst of ear-piercing laughter—mad, screaming laughter—that continued in paroxysm after paroxysm, till it would seem that human lungs could hold out no longer. After that there was silence again.

Crook and Merrick stared at each other, puzzled and amazed. Then suddenly came from above a flood of rapid, incoherent and high-pitched words, not one of which could be clearly distinguished; and again the loud sobbing sigh that had first startled them. And through it all there was a strange, unpleasant, almost unbearable tone of demoniac hilarity.

"Like all the yells in an insane asylum squeezed into one," whispered Merrick; and even as he spoke the laughter came again—in choking, uproarious fits— horrible, ghastly fits.

"What's this doing up above?" Merrick exclaimed, awe-stricken. "We can't stop and hear such sounds. Shall we knock?"

Crook laid his hand on his companion's arm, and

listened again. There came a long ripple of chuckles, growing louder and louder, and in the end changing into a burst of high, tuneless singing—such singing as might come from a man on the rack, in his delirium.

"There must be at least three men in there," said Crook; "but that is all one voice, and the others are silent. We'd better not wait any longer. What the matter is I can't guess, but even if it is the diamond we must risk it. I'll stay. You go downstairs at your hardest and bring Wickes from New Scotland Yard. Jump into the first cab—it's close by, but lose no time —and bring more than one man. Say we've got Pooley here, of course."

Another burst of laughter came as Merrick started on his mission, and the sound hastened his steps. Crook stayed behind to listen, while from above sounds succeeded sounds of unnatural hilarity, punctuated by dead silences. Crook began to wonder why the other tenants were not disturbed.

Mr. Merrick hustled as he had never hustled before, and though the time seemed long to Crook he was back in less than ten minutes, with Wickes and two assistants. Crook met them on the stairs, and together they ascended the top flight.

Even as they did so, the door before them opened, and Pooley stood before them, bag in hand. He sprang back instantly, but Wickes sprang too, and held the door open.

"Ah!" said Wickes heartily, "good morning, Robb —or Pooley, which you please! And Wide James, too —I think we must take you both along. And who is the happy old party?"

In an easy-chair before a table a short man, with a distinctly Jewish face, rolled and lolled and chuckled, his eyes wide open, but his brain unconscious of all that passed. On the table stood the magnum of Tokay, with three glasses; and a safe in the corner stood open, with papers spilt before it. Once again the man in the chair burst into his screaming laugh, and then relapsed into silence.

"That's the game, is it?" said Wickes, pointing to the bottle. "All right. I must trouble you for your wrists. Reeves—you'd better fetch a doctor."

The state of the case began to dawn on Crook and Merrick. This was the use to which the Tokay was to

be put—to drug a man into helplessness while his safe
was rifled with his own keys. And Crook saw at once
why Pooley had bought the Tokay as an instrument of
business, for a drug that would be detected in more
familiar drink would be taken readily in so rare and
unaccustomed a wine as Tokay, whose flavour would
probably be unknown to the victim.

Presently the doctor arrived, and after a sniff or
two at a glass pronounced the words "Indian hemp—
and something else with it."

That told more. Pooley had brought the drug from
India, and it was a drug in which the famous Indian
hemp—*bhang* or *hashisch*—had the chief part; the drug
that brings on laughing, yelling, happy delirium, and
leaves its victims broken and exhausted. It grew plain,
in fact, that it was the need of some likely drink in
which to administer the stuff that led Pooley to speculate
in the Tokay.

At first it seemed difficult to understand how the
three could have drunk together and only one suffer
from the drug. But a further discovery made that
plain. For the stuff was contained in a little rubber
ball with a protruding spout, which Pooley could hide

in his palm, and so doctor a glass of wine or not, as he pleased, while he poured it out. The experiments which Crook had witnessed through the window were no more than the tasting and testing that were necessary to judge of the practicability of the scheme. Isaacs had readily assented to the suggestion to try a glass of the rare wine which Pooley had with him, and so the thing was done.

No diamond was found in the bottle, nor anywhere about Pooley and his new lodgings. He had got to work quickly enough after his return, and on a likely victim. For, indeed, when Isaacs came to himself, very sick and wretched, he was as terrified at his predicament as was Pooley himself. For, as a matter of fact, the bonds which the scoundrels were about to carry away were stolen bonds already! So that Isaacs's troubles only began with the robbery; and as the law is usually severe on a receiver, they are not quite finished yet.

VI.

A BOX OF ODDMENTS.

I.

AFTER the adventure which made it plain that the mystery of Mr. Pooley's magnum had nothing to do with the missing green diamond, some little time was consumed by Harvey Crook and Mr. Merrick in unsuccessful attempts in different directions. Harvey Crook returned to Southampton, and with the aid of Mr. Symons, the auctioneer's clerk, succeeded in wasting some days in a futile pursuit of the magnums of Tokay still left unaccounted for. Merrick also went to Southampton, but it was for a shorter time, and his object was to learn what had been done by the police toward the apprehension of Pritchard, the murderer of his old friend, Mr. Clifton.

Crook left Southampton and regained London, with an idea of finding Smith, the wine-merchant's traveller, who had bought the four magnums of Tokay, or his employers. Crook was by no means certain that the firm belonged to London, but he could see no better way of setting to work than to make persistent inquiries at the offices of the principal firms by the aid of the London Directory. He made his list, and began what promised to be a very wearisome search. The first day was almost wholly wasted in a tedious pursuit of the wrong Smith. For, in fact, one of the first firms he tried chanced to employ a traveller of that name, who, being discovered after a hunt of several hours, was found not only to be a total stranger to Southampton, which was not in his district, but also a total stranger to Imperial Tokay, a liquid of which he knew nothing except by repute. The probability had already struck Crook that there might be several wine-merchants' travellers about of the name of Smith, and now he realised the difficulty to the full.

He ended his day's search in the vicinity of Euston Station, and he was emerging into the main road when he felt himself caught by the arm.

"Well, and what's your luck with the Eye of Goona?" asked a voice at his elbow.

The speaker was a rather tall man in a rather curious combination of garments. He wore a new tie-over coster's cap, an old bobtail coat, and excellent new trousers and boots. He had a blue choker where his collar should have been, and in his hand he carried a brown paper parcel. It was a disguise, no doubt, of a sort, but it did not serve for an instant to conceal from Crook the identity of Lyman W. Merrick, of Merricksville, Pennsylvania.

"Hullo!" answered Crook. "Luck? None at all —none. But why this get-up?"

"That's the disguise," replied Merrick, with some pride. "Rather a neat idea, I reckon, eh? I did try the red whiskers at first—got 'em put on at a theatrical place at Covent Garden—but they made my face itch stampin'-mad, and I just dragged 'em off as soon as I could get to hot water. Yes—crape-hair they called it, and I don't want any more of it, sir—not me. But see—you'll come and dine with us, won't you? We'll call a cab, and I'll undisguise."

The cab was called, and Mr. Merrick positively beamed as he revealed the inner cunning of his disguise.

"There's pretty considerable of a difficulty, you see," he explained, "in usin' a disguise when you're livin' at a hotel. You attract suspicion goin' in an' out dressed like a tough, with varyin' colours in the whiskers. So I've just fixed it up like this. See?"

He cut open the brown paper parcel, and took therefrom a neat light overcoat and a crush hat. He put on the light coat over the old bobtail, buttoned it, stuffed the cap into a pocket, opened the crush hat, and planted it on his head. Then he turned triumphantly to Crook.

"How's that?" he asked. "The brown paper and the string I contribute toward the support of the cabman by stampin' it down on the floor and leavin' it there. You'd never allow I'd been disguised now, would you?"

Crook was tempted to tell his friend that as a matter of fact he hadn't been disguised before, but Merrick's delight in his idea was so obviously sincere that Crook refrained from spoiling it. Instead he asked for news.

"I've told you I've had no luck," he said, "and I begin to despair of it. I seem to be wasting my time.

But as to you—why this mysterious disguise? After Pritchard, I suppose? Can you report better luck than I?"

Merrick shook his head.

"Well, no," he said, "I can't. Not yet. I must admit that what's been done as yet the police have done. They've traced Pritchard to London—or they think so."

"Come, this is news to me. Tell me about it."

"Well, they've been pretty active, and it seems that on the night of the murder, when he escaped from the house, he must have bolted out into the country, away from Southampton. They could find no trace of him at Southampton, but after a good deal of inquiry they found that a man corresponding to his description took a ticket for London at Shawford, a little station nine or ten miles from Southampton, early the next morning, and travelled up by the first train, leaving Shawford at 6.32. What he'd been doing in the meantime they can't guess, but they haven't found that he took a bed anywhere, so that it seems very likely he was out all night. Well, that was all they could get at for a little while. Of course all the ports are being watched, and so forth. But after our little adventure with 'Wide James' and Robb,—or Pooley as he was called on the *Rajapur*,—after that little scramble in the alley near Charing Cross, Sergeant Wickes came unexpectedly on what looked like a trace. But they've got no farther with it, nor have I."

"What was the trace?"

"Well, of course you remember that when the police had rescued Isaacs from the other two, they discovered that he was just about as tough a subject as they were themselves. All the bonds, in fact, that they had planned to steal were stolen bonds already. Now the police followed up that matter, and it grew plain that Isaacs had been carrying on a pretty big trade in stolen bonds and other valuable property—about the biggest in London, in fact. They made inquiries of some fellow in their pay—what they call a 'nark,' I think—who told them the names of several people who had been frequenting Isaacs's office, beside the two who had gone to rob him. And some o' them whose names he didn't know he described. One of them was quite a new arrival, and it struck Sergeant Wickes that it sounded a bit like the description of Pritchard. So he communicated with Southampton, and they sent up a photograph of Pritchard that they had managed to root out somewhere; and when their spy saw that he identified it positively!"

"Phew! Come, this looks like business!"

"Yes, so it seemed. But it's led no farther as yet. The police won't tell me what they are doing—they seem to think I may spoil their game, I believe!"

"And you haven't had any luck on your own account?"

"Well—no, I can't say I have. But I can't sit and do nothing, you see, so I'm watching out generally all day in this disguise. I've watched about the place at Charing Cross, but that don't seem very useful—the place is blown on now, you see. So this afternoon I came along here and looked around the neighbourhood where we saw those two toughs dosing up their bottle of Tokay; I wondered if *they* might be connected any way with Pritchard. It's slow work, and I don't seem to be doin' much, I allow. But I'm going to do my little best, foolish as it may be, and I'm watchin' out!"

Crook was thoughtful for a few minutes. "There is something in all this," he said at length. "Why should Pritchard go to Isaacs? We know all that he was supposed to have taken from Mr. Clifton's safe— sixty or seventy pounds' worth of notes and gold. He wouldn't need to go to Isaacs to sell *that,* would he?"

"No, he wouldn't. You're thinking of that green diamond, I guess."

"I am. It was in one of those dozen bottles, and I have already seen some of them opened without find- ing it. Also, it is not in the bottle you have. But we both found an unaccounted-for bottle already opened at Mr. Clifton's after the murder. I really think this is worth following up."

"Better than your own tack?"

"My own tack leads me nowhere just now. And I doubt if it's worth following much farther, in any case. You see the odds are that by this time the rest of those bottles have been opened. People who buy just a single magnum of such a rare old wine as that don't keep it very long before opening it; and I think it's more than likely that somebody has discovered that

13*

green diamond before now.   If it is some unknown
person, it is of little use for me to carry my search
farther.   If Pritchard has had it there may be a
chance."

"Even if he has already parted with it to Isaacs?"

"Even then, perhaps.   But here we are at the
hotel."

Mr. Merrick gave an extra stamp on the brown
paper, and emerged from the cab in most respectable
guise, to the astonishment of the driver; and in two
minutes Harvey Crook was shaking hands with Daisy
Merrick, who was no doubt quite as glad to see him as
she looked—perhaps even more so.   Though, after all,
a few days is not so long to be parted from a friend—
an ordinary friend—is it?

Daisy pushed across the table to her father a small
square parcel-post packet, which he took and examined
with some little surprise.

"It came soon after lunch," she explained.

"Well," he said, "I wasn't expecting anything, and
I didn't suppose I had any friends in this country to
send me little presents—unless some sportsman who

bought a magnum of my wine should think it only the fair thing to send me back the green diamond, eh?"

He tore away the paper cover, and came on a small wooden box. This he opened, and tumbled out on the table an odd little assortment of seeds, cloves, pieces of glass, a cork, and similar rubbish.

"What's this?" asked Merrick, staring. "This is just a fool-parcel. If it was the first of April I'd understand it, though I don't know who'd go to the trouble of fooling me that way, in this country, anyhow. But it *isn't* the first of April, and here is the fool-parcel all the same!"

"Isn't there a letter?" asked Daisy.

"No sort of a letter at all." He turned over the brown wrapping paper and shook the little box. "Nothing but this stuff."

Harvey Crook bent over the table. "May I look at it?" he asked.

"Of course—if it will amuse you. There it is—a chip of marble, a cork, a bit of green. glass, a bit of brass, a dead tulip-flower and the seeds. What do you make of that?"

Crook looked closely over the strange collection, and then picked up the little box and smelt it.

"Sandalwood," he said laconically. "This is Indian."

"Indian?"

"Yes—let me count those seeds. Have you got a newspaper, or something white?"

Daisy brought a napkin from the sideboard and spread it on the table. Crook transferred to its white surface the contents of the sandalwood box, being especially careful not to leave behind as much as a single seed. Then he began arranging the various objects before him, grouping each of its kind together.

"First," he said, "we have a piece of green glass. Then a cork from a bottle. Then the tulip; a red tulip, you see—blood red. Then there are ten cloves and eighteen other seeds, all the eighteen of one sort; they look like hemp-seeds, though perhaps they are something else. And to end up we have a chip of marble, such as you might pick up in any mason's yard, and a little piece of brass pipe. Mr. Merrick, you said there was no letter in this packet, but you were wrong. This *is* a letter!"

"A letter?"

"Yes, a letter. An Indian object-letter, though, as you see from the post-mark, it has been sent from a London post-office, in the West Central district. What is more, unless I am vastly mistaken, it is concerned with the Green Eye of Goona! Come — this gives furiously to think, as the French say."

"But I don't understand. What——"

"One moment. I don't understand either, just yet. But I think perhaps I can learn a little, with consideration."

"But if these things mean a letter, and a letter about that green diamond, why does it come to me?"

"There's a bottle of that Tokay in your luggage. Perhaps the sender thinks the stone is there. As to the things meaning a letter, I think that's pretty plain. This is a well-known means of communication among the natives in India, when they have anything to say that it wouldn't be safe to put into plain words. But I must think this over."

At this moment Daisy turned to shut the drawer in the sideboard, and Crook seized the occasion to make a quick signal to her father. He pointed to the

door, and then downward; and Merrick understood at
once that he wished to speak to him out of Daisy's
hearing.

"Dinner's at half-past seven," said **Mr.** Merrick,
"and there's nearly an hour. Daisy 'll want to dress,
I reckon, and I know I want a shave. If you want to
think over that boxful of notions, I guess you can do
your thinking pretty well anywhere?"

"Yes, I'll come with you," Crook answered, "of
course. We'll put the things back in the box, if you
like—now I know what they are. But these object-
letters require a rare exercise of the imagination before
their meaning is to be got at."

Once they were well clear of Merrick's suite of
rooms the American turned and said, " Well? And what
is it all?"

"What it seems to mean, in the first place, is that
more people are after this diamond than I have supposed. There are Indian natives after it, and they have
followed the clues pretty closely. Now who are they?
Are they sent by the Rajah to recover it, or are they
men who are in the secret of its disappearance and
wish to get it for themselves? Does Hahn know about

them, and if so, are they working with him or against
him? All these questions are matters of doubt. What
is no matter of doubt, however, is that these fellows
seem disposed to go to great lengths to get the jewel.
That letter, as I read it, is something very much—or
quite—like a threat of murder!"

Merrick whistled and stopped. *"Me?"* he asked.

"Well," Crook replied, "I'm afraid it looks like it,
since the packet was addressed to you, and that is why
I wouldn't offer my translation before your daughter. It
is likely they may have learned of your second purchase
of that magnum you have by inquiries of McNab, the
steward. But as to the package, just go over those objects in your mind, now. There was the piece of green
glass—broken from a stopper, I should think. That
must mean the diamond—I see no other meaning for
it, if the letter deals with the diamond at all. And the
cork means that they know it is in a bottle of wine—
by implication, also, that they know you have one of
the bottles. Then there is the red tulip. Now, in India,
in such messages as these, a red flower means danger
or death, if the sense of the accompanying articles
permits of it. There may be other secondary meanings,

if the flower appears in conjunction with certain other things, or with other flowers. But here it is alone, and it must bear its primary meaning. After that there are the seeds—of two sorts; cloves, and those others that look like hemp-seed. Now these seeds may have meanings of their own when they appear singly—probably they have. But when a number of such things are pitched in together they must always be counted; they mean nothing but figures. You will remember there were ten of the cloves and eighteen of the seeds. There we get the figures ten and eighteen. Do they suggest anything to you?"

"No, they don't, unless it is—well, to-day is the eighteenth of the month."

"Precisely. And that is just what I believe those eighteen seeds mean, from the context. Just consider, now. They begin by suggesting that you have the green diamond—the Eye of Goona—in your bottle, and that something unpleasant will happen to you in consequence. In other words, they want you to give it up. But how are you to give it up, and to whom? They must fix time and place. I believe those cloves and seeds represent the time, and since the eighteen seeds cannot represent an hour, they probably mean a day of the month—especially, remember, as these people are no doubt in a hurry, and to-day is the eighteenth. That being so, the cloves would tell the hour—ten. In fact, now I think of it, I am certain that I have heard of cloves being used before to indicate the hour in these letters. There you have it, then. You are to give up the Green Eye of Goona at ten o'clock to-night. Not very long notice, I'm afraid."

Mr. Merrick turned away from the barber's door and walked out of the hotel.

· "This is all square?" he asked. "You ain't pulling my leg?"

"Indeed I'm not. The thing seems grotesque enough to you, no doubt. But in India the object-letter is a matter pretty well known among those at all acquainted with native ways. The idea has been used here, that is all."

"Very well. Then I understand that they want the diamond—which I haven't got—and they threaten me unless I hand it over at ten to-night. Where?"

"That brings us to what seems in some ways the oddest part of the message. There is a grotesque in-

congruity about it, as I read it, which is quite fantastic.
And yet that very fact tells us something about the
person who made up the letter.   See now, we have
dealt with every object in the package but two—a chip
of marble and an inch of thin brass pipe.   Perhaps as
a stranger you are ignorant of some of the later Cockney
slang terms—more so than the person who sent this
package.   But surely you can guess something of the
meaning of those two little objects?   The piece of
marble, now.   Doesn't that suggest a notable spot in
London?"

"Not unless—why, you don't mean the Marble
Arch?"

"I do; and that is what I think the sender of this
letter means too, especially when the thing is considered
in conjunction with the other object going with it.   What
is it?   A tube!   Haven't you heard the new Central
London Electric Railway called the Tube?   And
on that line is the Marble Arch Station.   That is
the place meant—the Marble Arch Station on the
Tube!"

Mr. Merrick stared for a moment, and then
laughed.

"Yes," Crook assented, "it sounds a little odd, no doubt; but there it is, and if you can think of a better interpretation of the letter I wish you would; I can't. For the thing *is* a letter, without a doubt. And note this also. This chip of marble and the little piece of brass tube would scarcely be used as a direction by a person unfamiliar with London, would they? Inference: the Indian native who wants that diamond is either himself familiar with London or is in confederation with another who is."

"But—but—why shouldn't they write an ordinary letter? The address is written well enough and clearly enough in English. Why not the letter?"

"Again I think that tells us something. That letter, written in plain English, would be a demand with threats—a thing the police could and would take action on, if you brought it before their notice. As it is, it is a mere jumble of odds and ends which no police officer or magistrate would bother to look at twice. If you were to complain of a threat contained in such a form as that you would be regarded as a lunatic. It is an artfully protected intimation. Now this suggests that the sender knows something about the English law in this matter, and means to avoid risk."

"But how are they to know I would tumble to all their hocus-pocus? Because without your help I should never have guessed what the stuff meant."

"Not as matters are, perhaps. But suppose you *had* found that great green diamond in your magnum of Tokay: don't you think you would have suspected the meaning of the message then? I think you would. With the worry of that enormous possession on your mind, your doubts as to what to do with it, and what measures some unknown person might be taking to re-cover it, I think the receipt of that packet would strike you as a very significant thing, and you would have at least arrived at some vague idea of its purport."

"And if I didn't, then somebody would kill me, eh? As I suppose they will try to do now?"

Harvey Crook shrugged his shoulders. "Perhaps not that," he said, "at any rate just yet. I think if they got no satisfactory reply to this letter they'd probably follow it up with another a little more explicit —a few sketches, perhaps, designed to make their meaning plain to the meanest intelligence, so to speak.

This is little more than a hint—a hint being safer than anything more explicit. But the hint seems pretty plain to me, and I think we had better answer this letter."

"How?"

"That is not over-easy. It is a far simpler thing to decipher one of these letters, if you have a guiding clue or two, than to devise one which shall be clearly understood by others—especially if you are not in the habit of conducting your correspondence in that way. I think we will turn up at the Marble Arch Station at ten, and hand back the box to whoever applies for it. Inside the box we will put a little half-ounce bottle—we can get one at a chemist's—tightly corked, and empty. Outside the box, though inside the enclosing paper, we will put their little bit of green glass. That ought to express the fact that the jewel is not only not in your bottle, but is quite outside your knowledge. And you shall write it in words, if you like, as well. We haven't any particular reason for secrecy, you know, except that the more we tell them about where the diamond is *not,* the nearer they may be getting to where it is."

"Well," observed Merrick, as he turned toward the

barber's at last, "here is an adventure, at any rate; and that's what I've been asking for!"

II.

DINNER went pretty quietly, and Daisy Merrick was anxious to know what so fully occupied the minds of her father and his guest. She was told, readily enough, that the object-letter was supposed to be a demand for the Green Eye of Goona, which the sender obviously imagined might be in Merrick's possession; but nothing was said about any implied threat. And, dinner finished, the return parcel was made up as Crook had suggested.

"So much for the fool-puzzle," observed Merrick; "and now, if they can read English, here is a piece of it for them."

And he took a sheet of notepaper and inscribed on it in large letters:—

"Mr. Lyman W. Merrick begs leave to inform the gentleman who mailed him this box that he carries no jewels that do not belong to him, and that the only bottle of wine he has in this country contains nothing but the wine, if that is what the gentleman is driving at. Mr. Merrick has pleasure in giving the gentleman full permission to go and chase himself."

The note was packed into the box with the little phial, and the whole thing neatly sealed. Then the two men left for the Marble Arch Station.

"We shall look a rare fool-pair if nobody turns up to ask for this packet," Merrick observed with a laugh as they crossed Cavendish Square. "The thing seems a shade ridiculous, after all, here in Cavendish Square, London. Don't it?"

"Well, we shall see," Crook replied. "If nobody comes there's no harm done, and nobody to laugh at us but ourselves. I think, when we come to Oxford Street, we had better walk apart. You take the packet and keep on this side of the way, and I'll cross to the other. It's pretty certain they know you by sight, since they know where you are staying, and if anybody dogs or watches you, I can watch him, unobserved."

So they walked along Oxford Street, Merrick on the north side, Crook on the south. They had purposely

delayed their departure till the last moment, and ten
o'clock struck as Merrick was crossing the end of Port-
man Street. As the American strolled leisurely into the
light of the station Crook crossed the road, with his
eyes wide open for what might happen.

There, sure enough, in the middle of the door to
the booking-office stood a short, muffled man, a native
of India, unmistakably. Merrick walked calmly past
him, and the man turned, with a quick, nervous glance,
and followed him into the booking-office. A cab was
standing by the kerb, and Crook took a position in its
shadow and watched.

Merrick turned sharply and confronted the Hindoo,
who instantly made a nervous bow, looking inquiringly
into his face.

"My name," said the American, "is Lyman W.
Merrick, stayin' at the 'Langham.' Did you come here
to see me?"

The man bowed again, more nervously than before,
with a quick glance over his shoulder. Plainly he was
a timid conspirator, and from that nervous glance Crook
inferred that he must have a confederate near at hand.
Might that confederate be Hahn?

"Expectin' to receive a parcel, maybe?" asked Merrick.

The man bowed once more, with a low-voiced assent. And then at last Crook saw the confederate. It was not Hahn, but another Indian, bigger in build than the man in the booking-office, and clearly of another and stronger race. He stood in shadow near the door, an unregarded newspaper crushed in his hand, and his face thrust eagerly forward to watch. Crook had seen the man when he first crossed the road, but he had feigned to read his paper, and it was only now that his excited movement had allowed his dark, aquiline face and bristling moustache to become visible. It was a face, too, that somehow seemed oddly familiar to Crook, though he could in no way associate it in his memory with the frock-coat and tall hat which the man now wore.

"There's the parcel," said Merrick, placing it in the hand of the small man before him; and Crook saw the other Indian start visibly. "There's the parcel, with a note in it. I don't know what you mean, but if you mean what I guess you mean, you'll know what _I_ mean when you open that parcel. Savvy? I haven't got

14*

what you're after, sonny Snowball, and you'd better try
the next store."

The small man scarcely stopped to bow again, but
scuttled out hurriedly. As he passed the watcher by
the door the latter snatched eagerly at the parcel in
his hand, and the two together vanished into the
night.

Crook came from his lurking-place and rejoined
Merrick. "The man," he said thoughtfully, "the other
man—there was another outside whom I've certainly
seen somewhere. Where? Probably at Delhi; but there
I saw thousands. Still, I remember him in particular,
and—why, yes! I know! It was! It was Mehta Singh,
who was Chief Minister to the Rajah of Goona!"

"The same that was said to have cut down the
thief who had almost got away with the green diamond?"

"Yes, the same! He did cut him down, in fact.
Now, just consider that! The stone found in the dead
thief's hand was found to be a mere worthless crystal.
Now, did Mehta Singh kill his own confederate, or tool,
as soon as he had succeeded in getting the jewel, and

did he make the exchange when the wretched creature was dead? Was that his plan for stealing the diamond and at the same time gaining credit for faithful vigilance? And was Hahn at his back through the whole transaction? Do the facts suggest anything else —*can* they suggest anything else, indeed?"

The two men walked back along Oxford Street in deep thought. Presently Crook burst into a laugh.

"There's fun in it after all," he said. "I saw the way Mehta Singh snatched at that package, and I verily believe he thought the Green Eye of Goona was in it! He couldn't hear your talk, of course, any more than I could myself. And even if he could, he may not understand English. It will fall to the lot of that poor little Babu, his employee, to inform him that you have politely told him to—chase himself! I should dearly like to hear his rendering of that phrase in their vernacular!"

III.

HARVEY CROOK was curious, and something more than curious, to know if any reply would be vouchsafed to Merrick's packet-message, and for that reason he called at the Langham Hotel the next morning at about eleven—as, indeed, he had arranged to do before parting with Merrick at night. Nothing whatever had been received, and Mr. Merrick showed some signs of restlessness at the break in his daily hunts through London. Daisy Merrick was making preparations for a shopping walk, and her father was discussing the question as to whether he should go with her or not, when a message did arrive for Merrick—not at all of the sort they had been looking for. For it was a telegram in these words:—

Can you communicate with your friend Crook to come immediately eight Redway Street Gray's Inn Road possibly identify Pritchard. *Wickes.*

"Got him!" shouted Merrick, pushing the telegram into Crook's hands and rushing for his hat. "Come! you're the man, Crook! What could have been better!"

Crook read the words with some excitement himself, but scarcely with Merrick's enthusiasm.

"We won't be sure just yet," he said, as he prepared to follow his friend, "but we'll see. At any rate, I think I can identify him if they *have* got him. My memory of that night at poor old Clifton's house is certainly strong enough for that!"

No cab in London could have been fast enough for Merrick that day. The one they employed was really quite a brisk turn-out, but it took something almost like force on Crook's part to restrain his friend from getting out and hailing some other cab half-a-dozen times.

"The odds are we'll only get into a slower cab," Crook protested, "and we shall lose time changing. This horse is really smart, and after all, *if* they've got Pritchard, you may be pretty sure they won't let him go before we come." And so in the end Merrick was persuaded to sit still, if not quiet.

Redway Street, Gray's Inn Road, might almost have been another part of Meldon Street, Euston, to which their last adventure had led them, except that Redway Street seemed to have reached a shade lower level in the down grade from complete respectability. At one or two houses children played on the steps, and the cards announcing "apartments" were as often as not home-inscribed in ill-assorted capital letters.

At number eight a little wondering group stood by the area railings, and a policeman was on the top front step guarding the door. Plainly a rumour of "something up" was pervading Redway Street, though nobody quite knew what. Matrons with brooms stayed their work to talk and stare at number eight, and straggler after straggler stopped to increase the group at the gate.

"We'll keep the cab in case we want it again," Crook said; and the two men sprang out and up the steps of the house.

"Sergeant Wickes?" asked Merrick hurriedly; and the policeman at the door stood aside to let them pass.

Wickes met them in the passage, bony, square, clean-shaven, and matter-of-fact as ever.

"Good morning, gentlemen," he said; "you've been quick. I didn't expect you so soon. I haven't been here much over an hour or so myself. I suppose you'd have no difficulty, Mr. Crook, in identifying Pritchard if you saw him?"

"No—I think not."

"Even if he were dead?"

"Dead?"

"Yes, dead. Whether the man we have here is Pritchard or not I can't say, though it's likely; but dead he is, Pritchard or not. His throat's cut."

Crook and Merrick stared in amaze.

"I thought I'd mention it, you see," the detective said with business-like cheerfulness, "in case it gave you a shock when you went into the room. These things do shock some people, you know. Come this way."

They walked, with involuntarily hushed footsteps, to a back room, where on a common iron-framed bed a dead man lay, dabbled and terrible. The last time Crook had stood before such a sight was in Mr. Clifton's house, where this man's double crime had been committed. For Pritchard it was, as Crook could see at a glance. Grey and grisly he lay there, but scarcely greyer than he had been when Crook first saw him in the hall of Downs Lodge; and his face seemed strangely commonplace and peaceful—almost grotesquely so by contrast with the fearful wound that lay below, and the dabbled bedclothes that lay about it.

"Been dead since about three or four this morning, the doctor says," Wickes remarked. "You *do* identify him, then? Quite positively?"

"Yes—there's no doubt," Crook answered. "That is the man who received me that night at Mr. Clifton's house. Of that I am quite certain."

"Yes—I thought so," Wickes replied. "Not merely from the description, you see, which wouldn't be so much to go on for a man like me, who had never seen him alive, but because we have found one or two bank-notes with numbers corresponding to those missing from Mr. Clifton's safe. Mr. Clifton's bank people were able to do that for us, you see—a list of the notes."

"But who has done this?" Merrick asked.

Wickes shrugged his shoulders. "Can't say," he said. "Not yet, at any rate. The landlady found him like this when she came to do the bed. Thought he'd gone out. He's been going by the name of Neville here, it seems. The place hasn't been robbed, so far as I can see,—we found the bank-notes, as I told you. We've searched the place pretty closely, but everything seems quite ordinary, except two rather odd little packets that appear to have come by post. The odd thing about 'em is the way the address has been put on. See—here they are. Addresses made up of printed letters cut out of a newspaper."

The addresses on both packets were certainly strange. They were built up just as Wickes described, by capital letters cut from paragraph headings in newspapers, and pasted in proper order to make the words.

"Done to avoid betraying a handwriting, obviously," said Crook. "Anybody missing from the house?"

Wickes looked a little oddly at Crook. "You're not slow at these things," he said. "One lodger is out—an Indian, named Jatterji."

"Now look here," cried Crook suddenly, with a curious excitement. "One of those postal packets is flat and the other is square—a box, probably. See if

I can guess what you found in that box. A piece of green glass; a red flower; perhaps a cork—perhaps not——"

"No," interrupted Wickes quickly, "no cork!"

"No cork then, but a chip of marble, some cloves, some seeds, and a bit of brass tube!"

Wickes was plainly amazed. "So we did," he said. "But it seems to me you know more about this case than I guessed, Mr. Crook. We shall want to know all that!"

"Oh yes,—of course you shall know," Crook replied. "But first let me see the things for myself. You haven't lost any, of course. See, here are the cloves, Merrick—ten! And here are the seeds. Let us count. You had eighteen!"

They counted together. There were only seventeen seeds.

"That was a summons for the seventeenth!" exclaimed Crook. "And see the postmark—it was received on the morning of the seventeenth—a day before you got yours. Now let us see the other packet. That, you see, was delivered yesterday, the eighteenth, just as yours was. What is it?"

The second, and smaller packet, contained a sheet of paper with a rough drawing of a diamond on it, coloured green. Underneath were the words, again spelled out in letters cut from newspapers, BRING IT TO TUBE STATION MARBLE ARCH TO-NIGHT AT NINE IF YOU WISH TO SAVE YOURSELF.

"This is the second demand," Crook said. "More explicit, you see. What I said you would probably have received if you had taken no notice of the first. I should guess that Pritchard must have been terribly frightened at receiving the first, but he didn't quite tumble to its full meaning, and didn't know what to do. Then came the second, and he neglected that too—no doubt trying to invent some way of escape, and thinking to keep safe by staying indoors. You see, the time is just an hour before *your* appointment. They tried you, in the meantime, on the chance of the stone possibly being in your possession, and both shots failing—this was the result!" And Crook pointed to the figure in the bed.

They turned away, and Wickes came after them.

"You mustn't go, gentlemen," he said. "I must have an explanation of all this before you go. In an-

other room, of course, if you don't like this, but I must
have an explanation."

"Quite right—you shall," Crook replied. "Come
into another room and I'll tell you. But first do anything you can—wire or send or what not—to find Mr.
Jatterji, the lodger here. The odds are," he continued,
turning to Merrick, "he's the man you met last night—
Mehta Singh's assistant. You see he addressed *your*
packet in his own handwriting—it didn't matter. But
here—his writing might have been recognised, so he fell
back on the printed letters. We'll explain, Sergeant, as
soon as you please. But first, does the landlady give
you any information of value?"

"Nothing much. Pritchard has been here, under the
name of Neville, ever since he reached London, I should
say. He kept altogether to himself, and had no visitors.
This last day or two he shut himself completely up in
his room."

"Those packets were the reason for that," Crook replied, "and I think we can explain why. But it will
take a little time."

As a matter of fact, it took about twenty minutes,

at the end of which time Sergeant Wickes had the heads of the matter at command sufficiently well to write a very complete "docket" that evening. And the resources of Scotland Yard were turned to the tracing of Mr. Jatterji.

VII.

MR. SMITH'S MAGNUMS.

I.

DUNCAN MCNAB, chief steward of the *Rajapur,* was a man who, as we have seen, never allowed to pass an opportunity of making or saving a penny, or even the half of that sum. The thrifty care which kept him at his post on the ship at Southampton when he might have obtained leave, because leave would have meant not only a railway fare out of his own pocket, but payment for his own board and lodging, while remaining on duty would save both—that same thrifty care caused him rather to welcome than otherwise the delay in the repair of the *Rajapur.* For it meant a few more days free board and a few more days' pay to take—unless he were paid off summarily, which was not unlikely. But days went, no orders came, and he still remained, to his very great content.

It had been an uncommonly good voyage, on the whole, for McNab. Tips had been more plentiful and larger than usual, for it was not often that the *Rajapur* carried so many passengers of a well-to-do sort as she had carried on this last voyage, thanks to the Durbar and the overfilling of the mail-ships. And now, after profiting from the ship's good fortune in this respect, McNab was making a trifle more out of her misfortunes. Truly everything seemed going very well with McNab, and there was only one thing with which he was inclined to reproach himself—his lack of boldness in speculating in Tokay.

Plainly that had been a great chance lost. He had ventured so far as to speculate on a single magnum at the sale—and that with much misgiving that he was wasting his money. But this bottle, although it had only cost him nine shillings, had sold readily for five pounds, and McNab was consumed with angry regrets on two accounts—first, because he had not bought more magnums when he might have had them; and second, that he had not made Mr. Merrick pay more than five pounds for the one he had sold him. What it could be that made these magnums of wine so valuable McNab could not imagine; indeed he did not try, for he was far from being a man of imagination—he would have repelled that imputation with scorn. Certainly he never dreamed of such a reason as the concealment of a priceless jewel in one of the bottles. It was sufficient for McNab that here was quite a little crowd of people inquiring for those particular bottles of wine, and ready to pay high prices for them, too. In the first place, Mr. Merrick had given two hundred pounds for the dozen. That, figured the brooding McNab, was at the rate of £16, 13s. 4d. a magnum. True, he had immediately afterwards sold off eleven of the dozen at about nine or ten shillings apiece; but there was no accounting for the eccentricities of American millionaires, who could afford that sort of thing. Indeed, had not that same millionaire been glad soon afterwards to pay five pounds to get back one of the bottles? He ought to have been made to pay more—certainly he should have paid more, reflected McNab. There had been all sorts of people after that bottle since then, and he might have made his own price. Mr. Crook had been one of them—the man who had originally sold the dozen for two hundred pounds;

clearly *he* knew the value of the wine. Then there was a mysterious man—a foreigner, McNab supposed—the man whom Crook had afterwards described, and whom he had called Hahn. He had made higher offers than anybody—spoke casually of giving eight or nine pounds a magnum for any that he could get, and spoke in such a way that the shrewd McNab guessed very well that he would easily go higher. Lastly, the very auctioneer's clerk himself, one Symons, had found him out, and had offered first a sovereign and then two for the magnum he supposed he still had, or any other. Of course this offer McNab laughed to scorn; but it served at any rate to prove that the great value of this wine had become known to the clerk, who was anxious to make a profit out of his knowledge. Duncan McNab grew gloomy and savage. Why hadn't he had the enterprise of that fellow Smith, the man who had bought the next four lots after the first? He had paid ten shillings for each, and it was only that extra shilling that had choked McNab off the lot following the one he had actually bought.

Now early on the morning of Merrick and Crook's adventure at the late Pritchard's lodgings in Redway

15 *

Street, in London, McNab was taking an airing in Southampton, cogitating on these things, when he suddenly became aware of Hahn himself, standing on the steps of an hotel, smoking a cigar, and smiling and nodding recognition.

"Ah, Mr. McNab, how do you do?" cried Hahn with a very elaborate cordiality. "You don't remember me, do you? I called on you on your ship to inquire about some wine—you remember now, don't you? You had sold it, you know. My name is Hahn, and I came back to my hotel—this is my hotel—yesterday morning. Will you have a drink, Mr. McNab?"

This was an invitation to which McNab never failed to respond. Indeed if it were not for such invitations it would have been cheaper to be a teetotaller. So Hahn and McNab went into the bar, and McNab drank whisky.

"Yes," pursued Hahn, who seemed uncommonly— even feverishly — communicative — "yes, I came here early yesterday morning, and registered in the office just before twelve. I—I took a sitting-room, as well as a bedroom, and told them to book it from that time; and I had lunch here. I've been in the place, in fact, ever since. By the way, what's the day of the month?"

"Nineteenth," replied McNab.

"Yes, of course—Thursday the nineteenth. I might have known. I shouldn't have expected to find you in Southampton so long, Mr. McNab!"

McNab explained the reason of the delay.

"Ah—yes, most unfortunate," Hahn commented. "Most unfortunate. And yet if it had not been for that little accident I should not have have had the pleasure of meeting you here, Mr. McNab, on the nineteenth—Tuesday the nineteenth—after being at this hotel since midday yesterday, which was the eighteenth. So if you'll finish your glass, Mr. McNab, we will have it refilled! It all goes down in my bill, you see; I'm staying here, since yesterday morning,—the eighteenth."

McNab did not wholly understand Hahn's frequent references to the date and time of his arrival at the hotel, but he quite appreciated the whisky, not to mention the comforting reflection that he was a shilling ahead as a consequence of the encounter.

"I think you remember me now, Mr. McNab," Hahn resumed. "I offered you a good price for that bottle of

wine, you know, didn't I? Eight or nine pounds I'd
have given, or even a bit more, for that magnum of
wine, or any others like it. You've never seen any since,
have you?"

McNab shook his head gloomily. "I have not, Mr.
Hahn," he said. "Not a bottle whatever. You'll be
vairy fond of that Tokay wine, I'm thinkin'?"

"Oh yes, of course," Hahn replied. "As a collector,
of course. I'd give high prices for that particular case
of Tokay as a collector. I'm sorry you haven't been
able to get any for me, Mr. McNab. I don't think I
should have refused ten pounds a magnum, Mr. McNab.
As it is, I'm sorry, both for your sake and mine. You
might have made a good profit, and I should have been
very glad to get the wine."

This roused all the bitter regrets that the whisky
had tended to mollify; and presently, after listening to
a few more reminders that Hahn had been at the hotel
since yesterday morning, and was very sorry to have
missed the Tokay, McNab took his departure.

He walked through the town toward the dock, and
scarcely two streets from Hahn's hotel he found himself
in luck again. For, emerging from the private bar of a

public-house, he saw another person whom he recognised. It was a little man, round, oiled and brushed, with a red polished face, and large triangular checks all over his clothes. His body seemed positively globular on his neat little legs, his face was round, his cheeks were round, his low-crowned hat, perched aside, was all brimmy curves and curls and high polish, and his general fulness and roundness suggested that a very slight accident would cause him to burst like an over-ripe gooseberry. And in this nobby litttle man, McNab, with a shock of astonishment, recognised .Smith, the wine-merchant's traveller who had bought four magnums of Tokay at the sale!

The nobby little man went strutting along the street, and McNab went after him—not strutting, but galloping. Three seconds was time enough for McNab to recover from his surprise, three more to realise that here, within half a mile of each other, were the two men between whom a large profit was to be made, and —to catch Smith.

"Eh? Hullo!" ejaculated the little man, seized by the shoulder. "What's up?"

"Morrn', Mr. Smith! Maybe ye'll no remember me;

but I saw ye at the sale here at Lawson's a whiles ago, when ye bought four magnums of Tokay. I'm thinkin' maybe you're looking for a customer for they four magnums."

"No," answered Smith, "I ain't."

McNab's face fell. "Maybe they're sold?" he queried.

"No," Smith replied; "barrin' one. I did sell one. But I've got the others — an' got 'em 'ere in Southampton, too. As I said, I ain't lookin' for a customer. But I'm open to an offer. What'll ye give?"

"Fifteen shillun' a magnum," said McNab, with a wrench at his heart-strings. For indeed this man had bought them at ten shillings, and it was positively agonising to have to offer him more. "Fifteen shillun' a magnum; and that's a clear profit o' feefty per cent for you," the steward added with something like a groan.

"*That's* no go," said Smith decisively, with a cock of the hat and a turn in the direction of his journey. "I can do a lump better than that with 'em."

"Weel—don't go—ah'm no sayin' but what I might

revise the offer a trifle," urged McNab. "Say twa pun' ten for the three, then."

"That's a five-bob advance on the lot," replied Smith, whose arithmetic was as ready as McNab's. "Not a bit o' good—it's wastin' time. Ten pound for the three."

"Impawsible, Mr. Smith, quite impawsible!" gasped McNab in agony. "Sic an' awfu' sum is unreasonable!"

"All right—don't pay it," answered the implacable Smith. "You needn't, you know. *I* didn't ask you. But if you want them three magnums that's the price, without a penny of discount. Barring enough to pay for a drink," he added liberally. "I'm willing enough to stand that."

Poor McNab was shocked and amazed. That anybody but himself should contemplate making a large profit out of those magnums of Tokay seemed a wicked and deplorable thing. The notion of paying ten pounds for those three bottles racked him to the soul. And yet—he could make thirty pounds of them at the least, merely by carrying them down the street to Hahn's hotel. He made one last desperate attempt to secure an abatement, and then, finding that nothing would shake the adamantine Smith, he agreed.

"Very well," said the nobby little man calmly. "They're not far off.   Got the money with you?"

Yes, McNab had the money.   It was not McNab's habit to leave money or other valuables about in his cabin while the ship lay in dock.   He was ready to complete the bargain.

"All right, we'll go straight along," Smith said. "I'm stopping at Nottidge's—always do.   I left the magnums there when I bought 'em, knowing I'd be back in a little while before I went to London.   It ain't far."

They walked together to Nottidge's Hotel, Mr. Smith humming gaily as he went.   The little man was on Bob and Sarah terms with the entire household of Nottidge's, and the transaction was completed with very little ceremony.   McNab had his three big bottles, and Smith had his ten pounds.

"That's settled, signed, and sealed," said Smith as he dropped the sovereigns into his pocket.   "Now we'll go to the bar and get that drink I promised you.   I'll get Bob to do those bottles up in straw and brown paper, if you like, so that you can carry them. What'll you have?"

McNab glanced round the bar, and saw a list of American drinks, the topmost of which was priced at eighteenpence. So he had that. Whisky would have pleased him a great deal better, but would not have torn away half as much of Smith's ten pounds.

But Smith was quite cheerful. He paid for the drinks gaily, and sent the pot-boy to pack the magnums.

"That's no bad deal for me," Smith said. "Those four bottles cost me two pound, and I got the money back before I left the auction-rooms. Remember that murder the other day over there behind the town? Old gentleman named Clifton? Well, he bought one magnum of me. He bought one himself in the sale, and afterwards, as I was going out, he said he wished he'd bought another, and asked if I could spare one o' mine. 'Yes,' says I, 'at a price, o' course.' 'How much?' says he. 'Two pound,' says I; and he paid it without another word, though I fancy he looked a bit sour at being rooked. So I stood on velvet, you see. Them three o' yours cost me nothing."

This was a cruel rubbing of it into McNab. Mr. Clifton had looked sour at paying two pounds for a magnum—and now he, McNab the frugal, had paid ten pounds for three!

"So that between the two of you," Smith pursued, "I did very well. Very well indeed. All your ten quid's found money, you see, old chap! Not that I'd ha' let 'em go for much less; not very much less, anyhow. I might ha' knocked off a quid or two if you'd stood out, but as you didn't, that's neither here nor there."

McNab's inward writhings began to show in his face. Hahn should be made to pay for all this. No ten pounds a magnum to Hahn now!

The expensive American drink being finished, and the bottles tied up in a straw-packed parcel, McNab went off for Hahn's hotel with no delay. Smith strolled as far as the corner of the street with him, and there stood, watching his progress. As the little man stood there, Symons, the auctioneer's clerk, entered the hotel he had just left.

Now Symons had for some days been in pursuit of Smith by systematic means. A wine-merchant's traveller,

he argued, visiting Southampton, probably had cus-
tomers there. Therefore steady inquiry at Southampton
public-houses would probably yield information. Steady
inquiry he began, therefore, and this morning he had
learned that Mr. Smith, when in Southampton, usually
stayed at Nottidge's. Smith had had four bottles of
that Tokay, and since Symons could count on a profit
of five pounds a bottle from Crook, even if he paid
five pounds a bottle for the wine, the business-like
Symons hoped to make twenty pounds at least by an
interview with Smith.

So that presently, as the triumphant Smith saw
McNab disappear in the entrance of another hotel, he
was touched on the shoulder, and turned to confront
Symons.

"Good morning, Mr. Smith," said Symons. "My
name's Symons. You don't know me, but I think we
can do a stroke of business together. Shall we go back
to Nottidge's?"

So the nobby little traveller and the auctioneer's
clerk went back to Nottidge's.

II.

McNab, with the parcel of precious magnums hugged under his arm, found Hahn, with a fluttering telegram in his hand, busy at the hotel office. Turning away hastily therefrom, he almost knocked McNab and his weighty burden over.

"Aye, Mr. Hahn," said McNab, "ye see I'm no' so long awa'. Ye hae luck, Mr. Hahn,—I've three magnums o' the Tokay here!"

Hahn was curiously preoccupied and excited, but he controlled himself by an effort.

"No!" he cried. "You don't say so, Mr. McNab! Three magnums?"

"Oh aye, sir, three hail magnums o' the lot that was roupit at Lawson's. Ye shall hae 'em as reasonable as pawsible, Mr. Hahn,—though I paid cruel dear for 'em mysel'!"

Hahn looked at his watch. "And how much shall we say then, Mr. McNab," he said, "for the three magnums?"

"I'll juist tak' aff the wrappin's," said McNab, fencing the question for the moment. "I'll juist tak' aff, and ye shall see the bottles yersel'—fine an' great bottles as they are; fine great bottles."

"Never mind that," Hahn answered impatiently. "Don't bother about unpacking them. How much for the lot?"

McNab drew a long breath and looked hard in his customer's eye. "Feefty pun'," he said.

"Right!" Hahn answered hurriedly. "That'll do. I must run out to the bank and get the money. Sit down here in the hall, Mr. McNab, and wait. I may be gone a quarter of an hour or twenty minutes—perhaps a little more. But you'll be sure to wait, Mr. McNab, won't you?"

"Oh aye, I'll wait," answered McNab readily enough; and he found a seat while Hahn hurried out at the door.

It was a noble profit, but he was angry with himself nevertheless. He never expected Hahn to jump so willingly at such a demand, and now he was consumed with vexation not to have asked more. He might as well have said a hundred—at worst Hahn could only have offered less. But how could anyone have guessed that Hahn would pay such a sum? And at any rate fifty pounds for the three was the equivalent of the rate Merrick had paid for the whole case on the ship. But the consolation to be drawn from this fact was marred by the reflection that he, McNab, had sold this same Merrick a bottle for five pounds. It was a wicked thing, thought McNab, for a rich man to take advantage of him like that.

Hahn was a long time gone to the bank, but a prospective profit of four hundred per cent made McNab patient.

And he had the satisfaction of scoring over Smith too. For the steward had not long occupied his seat when Smith came puffing and hurrying in.

"Ah, here you are!" cried the nobby little man. "I thought this was where you came. I've come to do a deal. I'll give you a profit on your bargain over them magnums."

"Verra kind of ye, Mr. Smith," replied McNab sweetly. "What amount of profit would ye be disposed to offer?"

"I'll give," said Smith, "four quid a bottle."

McNab shook his head with quiet enjoyment. "Na, na, Mr. Smith," he answered. "It's no go, in your ain words. Twenty pun' a bottle might do it, now."

"Twenty? Pooh—nonsense. Look here—here you are; twelve sovereigns—no, I'll make it thirteen. Here you are, thirteen quid for the three!" And he rattled the money in his hand.

But McNab only shook his head again, and enjoyed the action. Clearly Smith had come to some sort of knowledge of the real value of this wonderful, this marvellous wine, in the last half hour. Perhaps—who could tell?—he had met Hahn outside, and Hahn had sent him to try to get the bottles cheaper. But that game wouldn't do with McNab. Hahn would have to come himself and pay the full fifty. No, no!

"Won't take it?" queried Smith shortly. "I shan't offer a cent more—I can't; wouldn't get anything out of it for myself if I did. You'll make more out of it than I shall, at that price. For the last time, then, will you take the thirteen?"

"For the last time, Mr. Smith," answered McNab with a smile of amused superiority,—"for the last time, I will not!"

The Green Eye of Goona. 16

"All right—keep 'em. No harm done!" And Smith slapped the money back into his pocket and strutted out.

Really Hahn was a long time at the bank—a very long time. McNab waited and waited. He had been there more than an hour now, and the hotel servants were beginning to take an inquisitive interest in him. Presently one of the porters, after taking instructions at the office, came across and said respectfully, "Was you a-waiting for anybody, sir?"

"Aye," answered McNab. "For Mr. Hahn."

"But Mr. Hahn's been gone an hour and more."

"Oh aye, I ken that verra weel. I'm juist waitin' till he comes back."

The man looked surprised. "But he's gone away, sir," he said. "Gone by train. He sent his luggage before you came."

"Eh? What? Gone by train? No—he's no gone by train. He tell't me he'd be back."

The man looked a little doubtful at this. "I'll send and ask the boots, sir," he said. "He took the luggage to the station."

The boots came, and testified not only that he had carried Hahn's bag to the station, but that he had

waited there and seen him go off by the twelve-ten train
for London. There was no doubt whatever about that,
the man said, with decision.

"He got a telegram," explained the porter, "and
ordered his bag down at once, sir. The boots went off
with the bag just afore you came in, and left Mr. Hahn
payin' his bill. I see him a-talkin' to you and a-lookin'
at his watch, and then he ran out an' caught the train.
Leastways boots 'ere says he caught it."

"Yes," corroborated boots, with all the affirmation
he could muster; "he caught the train—I see him catch
it. I see him catch it, certain, I did, with my own eyes,
myself!"

There was no getting beyond this, and the specula-
tive McNab began to experience an awful sinking in the
stomach. The telegram—he remembered seeing the
telegram in Hahn's hand. And now he remembered
that Hahn had been rather oddly preoccupied, and certainly he had been in a great hurry to get away—to the
bank, as McNab had fondly supposed.

The two hotel servants stood stolidly looking into the
steward's pallid face, till presently McNab gasped, "The
bank—which is Mr. Hahn's bank in the town?"

The porter looked at the boots and the boots looked at the porter. Then they shook their heads together.

"No bank, sir, not 'ere I should say. You see he don't live 'ere. He's only been 'ere once before—a little while back. But I'll ask at the office, if you like."

The man went over to the office and left McNab a few quiet moments wherein to absorb the appalling conviction that in some mysterious, wholly unaccountable fashion he had been—done; done. Then the porter came back, shaking his head once more.

"He always pays his bills in cash, sir," he said, "and did to-day, with a note from a roll of 'em. They don't think, in the office, as he has any bank 'ere."

"Notes?" gasped poor McNab. "A roll of notes? Was't a big roll of notes?"

"Can't say that, sir," the man answered. "They might know over at the office."

Over to the office McNab went, with the porter close by his elbow, and asked his question about the roll of notes, explaining that Hahn owed him money. The young lady in the office said that the roll of notes seemed a pretty large one—a hundred pounds or more, she felt certain. And at that information—that proof that Hahn could have paid on the nail if he had wished to do so—the heart of McNab sank into his very boots. He suffered himself, unresisting, to be gently shepherded into the street, and there he walked up and down hugging his hateful parcel in a daze of anger and despair.

No wonder Hahn had been so ready to agree to a price he never meant to pay. But then—why come after the wine in the first place? What did it all mean? And surely the whole thing could not be delusion? It was not only Hahn who wanted the wine—there was quite a crowd after it, all willing to pay well. And at that thought McNab's wits came back. There was Smith —he had offered thirteen pounds to buy the bottles back. Come, there would be *some* profit in this thing, anyhow.

III.

That morning, in London, after the return from the scene of the tragedy in Redway Street, Harvey Crook found this telegram awaiting him:—

"*Three magnums Tokay here, but may have to pay long price. How high may I go? Hahn here.*

Symons."

The Tokay interested Harvey Crook no more. The great green diamond had left its lurking place in the bottle bought by poor old Mr. Clifton, and was now in the hands of Mehta Singh, leaving a track of murder behind it. Of that Crook was certain enough; the tale he had heard of Pritchard's behaviour upon his receipt of the mysterious object-letter, of his shutting himself up in his room, obviously frightened, but clinging to the stolen jewel still, his previous visits to Isaac's office, and the rest of the whole matter,—these things left no doubt in Crook's mind. So that he resolved to instruct Symons to trouble no more about the wine. But the tail of the message was significant. Hahn was in Southampton—apparently, since Symons mentioned the fact, still trying to buy the wine. Indeed there seemed no reason why Symons should mention his name in connection with the possibility that a high price might have to be paid for the Tokay, except to suggest that Hahn's competition might raise the price. This would seem to indicate that Hahn was not in league with Mehta Singh, knew nothing of the actual situation of the Green Eye, nothing of the murder in Redway Street. The reflection gave Crook an odd sense of relief for which he would have found it difficult to give a reason. The man was a scoundrel, and Crook had no reason to love him; yet it was in some way a comfort to believe that he was not an accomplice in murder.

So Crook replied to Symons thus:—

"Buy no more Tokay of that lot. I will come down and explain. *Crook."*

Crook felt that some compensation was due to Symons for this sudden rescission of his orders, and for the trouble to which he had been put. So he decided to run down to Southampton and settle, while he had a few unoccupied hours.

It was because of Symons's receipt of this telegram from Crook that further tribulation fell on the head of McNab. When that Napoleon of commerce at last abandoned his forlorn perambulations before the door of the hotel which Hahn had abandoned, he made his best pace for Nottidge's. Smith was there, smoking a cigar half a foot too long for a man of his size, and writing a letter, in the commercial room.

"Mr. Smith," cried McNab, "I've changed my mind. I'll tak' your thirteen pun'."

Mr. Smith turned round in his chair and looked up at McNab with the cigar cocked up as though it were a pea-shooter directed at the steward's head. So he surveyed McNab for a moment, and then shook his head solemnly.

"It's no go—in my own words, as you said. No go, my cute friend!"

"No go! But surely ye stand by your offer, man?"

"I made my offer once, and you wouldn't have it. 'He that will not when he may'—you know that pretty little verse, don't you?"

"The twal' pun' then—surely ye'll gie twal' pun'?"

Smith's round, sleek head began shaking steadily again. "I'm quite sure I won't give you twelve pennies," he answered deliberately. "When I made you that offer, it wasn't for the sake of the wine, you may be sure, else I shouldn't ha' sold it you for what I did. I made that offer because I had a better one, and I could ha' made a quid or two out of it—and so could you. But that better offer's withdrawn now,—it's off. Consequence, I don't want the wine, and I'm perfectly satisfied with the transaction as it stands. *I've* done all right out of it!"

McNab was plumbing the very deeps of despair.

"But ye'll no leave 'em on my hands like this, Mr. Smith?" he pleaded. "Ye'll relieve me of some pairt of the loss, conseederin' the circumstances?"

"Considerin' the circumstances, I'll see you blowed first. Why should I take any of your loss? You'd ha' made a gain if you'd taken my offer,—and you grinned in my face when I made it! No, my boy. I'll tell you who it was made me the higher offer, if you like—the offer that's withdrawn. You can try him; go and give him a turn before I begin to get tired of you!"

"What's his address, Mr. Smith?"

"Symons, the clerk at Lawson's, auctioneers—up by the Memorial Hall. Where the stuff came from first."

McNab waited no more, but tore away to Symons with the fateful parcel in his arms. Symons was as tough as Smith. He had had an order for the wine, and now the order was countermanded; that was all. He wouldn't buy the three magnums, nor two, nor even one, at any price whatever. And he was most exasperatingly cheerful over the whole transaction; so that now at last, driven to utter madness, the unhappy McNab ranted and swore and danced on the office doorstep and proclaimed his wrongs aloud to all the world.

"It's a conspeeracy!" he cried. "A rank creeminal conspeeracy amang the hail gang o' ye, sendin' me frae ane to t'ither! A wicked conspeeracy to rob me o' my money! I'm robbit—robbit o' ten pun' by a haill gang o' thieving conspeerators!"

So that in the end, for the credit of the office, it grew necessary to call a policeman to propel the vociferous victim on his way. And so at last he went, and Symons saw him no more.

But McNab's talk of conspirators sending him from one to another, and the other glimpses of the day's doings which had been vouchsafed Symons, sufficiently aroused his curiosity to induce him to spend an hour in tracing the steward's adventures from Nottidge's to the other hotel and back again. So that when Crook arrived in Southampton that evening Symons was able not only to explain how Mr. Clifton came by his second magnum, but also to give him a pretty clear idea of the course of events during the day.

"Hahn came into the office twice—I don't know why," said Symons. "Once yesterday and once early this morning. He made casual inquiries about that Tokay each time, but didn't seem to care what I told him, or whether I told him or not. Not a bit so keen on it as he was before. But he seemed very anxious to bring himself to my recollection, and asked me each time if I remembered him. And he was particular, also, to tell me each time where he was staying, and that he'd been there since yesterday morning, the eighteenth, as he was careful to say. I don't know why he thought I wanted to know about his movements."

Crook also could not account for it till an idea struck him. And then the idea was that perhaps Hahn was not innocent of complicity in the murder of Pritchard after all.

For what could it mean, this anxiety to impress on a stranger his identity, the date, and the time of his stay in Southampton? What but a careful preparation for a later proof, if it were necessary, of his absence from London on the night of the eighteenth? In short, an *alibi?*

VIII.

THE GREEN EYE.

I.

Harvey Crook returned to London by the early morning train, busy with many thoughts. From what he had learned at Southampton it seemed probable—indeed, it grew clear—that beyond himself there was only one party of searchers after the great green diamond, and that Mehta Singh and Hahn were acting in alliance. Before the night when it had been planned that the wretched criminal Pritchard should be murdered for the sake of the jewel he carried, Hahn had been careful to travel to a place eighty miles distant from the scene of the tragedy, to remain there over the fatal night at an hotel where he was known, and to bring himself to the notice of anybody who could identify him. The object—to make ready for an *alibi*, should it be necessary—was apparent. Then on the following day,

on receipt of a telegram, he had returned to London by
the next available train. He had been waiting for that
telegram, it seemed, from the first thing in the morning,
and had inquired for it several times. So much Crook
learned by boldly inquiring for him at the hotel, and
then, on being told that he had gone to London, asking
if he had received a telegram. Now, what could have
been the purport of that telegram, and from whom
could it have come? From whom but Mehta Singh,
advising him of the successful accomplishment of the
crime? Everything pointed in the same direction. Hahn
had called at the auctioneer's office with inquiries as to
the bottles of wine, in one of which the jewel had
formerly been concealed; but, as Symons the clerk had
said, it was plainly more with the object of making his
presence in Southampton known than in any eagerness
after the Tokay, about which, in fact, he seemed
strangely indifferent by contrast with his earlier anxiety.
So that, on the whole, the thing was plain enough.
The murder was Mehta Singh's, with the aid of the
docile Jatterji, and, once it was well over, and his own
absence from the scene established in case of future
trouble, Hahn had hastened off to share in its profits.

The police must know this, Crook reflected, as soon
as he could convey the information to Inspector Wickes.
And with that reflection came another—that he must
give up the notion of himself recovering and restoring
the Green Eye to its lawful owner, the Rajah.   For if
the criminals escaped, the diamond would go with them;
and if they were taken, the police would seize the jewel.
And clearly Crook's energies, if they were to be exerted
in the matter, must be exerted on the side of the law.
On the whole Crook was not altogether disappointed;
for if he recovered the stone himself, and opened
negotiations from England for its return, he would be in
the not wholly worthy position of an unlawful possessor
demanding something like blackmail; and if he carried
it into India he would at best be dependent on the
Rajah's whim for his profit, and probably for his life, if
he ventured into the snug little native state of Goona
with that stone in his possession and no particular proof
—what proof could there be?—that he had not himself
been implicated in the original theft.

Now it is just possible that the risk of this adventure
might have attracted Crook six months ago.   But something had occurred meantime which had caused Harvey

Crook to look on many things with changed eyes. Possibly the reader may not have noticed it. Small blame be his if he has not. Even Mr. Merrick had not noticed it, in fact; but—and this was all that really mattered—Mr. Merrick's daughter had. More, her own view had undergone just so much modification that, whatever view she took of anything, Mr. Harvey Crook occupied the central and most important space in that view. So that while for Harvey Crook a journey East, of doubtful profit, every mile of which would carry him farther from Daisy Merrick, presented a singularly un-attractive prospect, that young lady's own private inclina-tions, had any supernatural means of penetrating them been available, might have been found ready to offer obstacles of their own.

So Crook, well reconciled to the prospect of losing a profit on the straying diamond, came to London with none the less desire to see it recovered from Hahn's clutches. For Hahn, it was plain, must have been the moving spirit in the theft from the beginning. He it was who had tricked Crook into accepting the risk of its transport to Europe, and there could be no doubt that it was he also who had devised the plan for its abstraction from the Goona treasures in the Durbar camp, and had supplied Mehta Singh with the false crystal found in the hand of their accomplice-victim, the professional thief, after Mehta Singh had cut him down.

Arrived in London while the morning was still young, Crook called a cab, with the idea of an instant visit to Sergeant Wickes at Scotland Yard. All down White-hall his cab followed another, which turned into the yard first, and as Crook alighted, he was surprised to perceive Mr. Merrick paying the driver of this first cab.

"I've come to worry Sergeant Wickes," explained Merrick. "I've got tangled up in this adventure so far, and I want to see it right through. I haven't seen Sergeant Wickes since we left him at Redway Street yesterday, and I want news, if there is any. He won't mind, will he?"

"Probably not," Crook answered, "especially as I have brought some information for him."

Wickes, by chance, was on the premises—in the act of leaving, in fact. He heard all Crook had to tell him with great interest. Yesterday's inquiries after the

Hindoos, he admitted, had led to nothing as yet, and he saw readily enough that Hahn might well supply another clue leading in this direction, if his movements after leaving Southampton could but be traced.

"We know the train he came by," Wickes said, thoughtfully, "and if he took a cab at Waterloo, we can find that too. I am immensely obliged to you, Mr. Crook. Meantime, gentlemen, I think I may show you this in confidence. It arrived by post, as you see, just now. Rather odd, I think."

He pushed an envelope across the table, addressed simply, "Police, New Scotland Yard, S.W." The address itself was laconic enough, but that was not what startled Merrick and Crook together, but the fact that the address was built up with capital letters, cut from newspaper headings, and pasted on the envelope—just as had been done with the envelopes found in Pritchard's room.

Crook took the envelope and opened it. Within was a sheet of paper inscribed in precisely the same way, in capital letters, cut from a newspaper, thus:—

REDWAY STREET MURDERERS, TWO INDIANS HIDING IN
OLD HOUSE, CORNER OF LARTER STREET AND ROOK STREET,
LAMBETH, CAPTURE QUICKLY.

"That is where I am going at once," Wickes said,
rising. "If you gentlemen are interested, there's nothing
to prevent you coming too—independently, of course.
You have seen the men, and may be able to identify
them, if they are there. I have just been making arrangements in the matter, or you would have missed
me."

Wickes and a brother officer went in a hansom, and
Crook and Merrick followed in another, perplexed and
expectant. What was the meaning of this odd communication to the police, and who could have sent it?
Was it a mere blind? That would soon be proved one
way or the other. And yet it seemed wholly unlikely.
If the guilty person were using such a communication
to put the police off the scent they would scarcely give
away the important fact that they were Indians; that, at
any rate, would be anything but a safeguard. And, in
any case, who could have sent the note? The curious
manner in which it was built up in printed letters of

course suggested the Babu Jatterji—it was precisely the expedient he had adopted a day or two ago to prevent the identification of his handwriting. But, although it was possible—even likely—that he might denounce Mehta Singh to save himself, would he denounce himself at the same time? There was no distinction made —the note spoke of two murderers. Further, if Mehta Singh and Jatterji were together, how could the Babu have found an opportunity to paste up this elaborate note unobserved? This consideration led to another conjecture. Could it be possible that there were three Indians altogether, two besides Jatterji, concerned in the crime? The postmark gave no help at all; that was merely "London, W.C."

The ride was a short one. Once over Westminster Bridge, the cab ahead traversed the main road for a little more than a quarter of a mile, then turned once to the left and again to the right, and then pulled up.

Wickes paid the cabman and walked back to Crook.

"This will be near enough," he said. "You can follow on foot. Of course, the place is watched from outside already—I saw to that at once."

Wickes and his companion walked smartly off, and

17 *

Crook and Merrick followed. The district was one which seemed to be in course of changing its character. Large manufacturing buildings were taking the place of small cottage-dwellings; such as remained being now squalid enough, though plainly at one time semi-rural, clean, and even sometimes picturesque. Here and there among the cottages a larger detached house stood, now either devoted to some sort of manufacturing purpose or standing blank and derelict. Through two or three such streets as these Wickes led the way, and stopped at the farther end of the last, where a stout hoarding enclosed a small piece of ground, vacant, except for a house at the extreme corner.

Much demolition was going on hereabout, and the street was almost bare of passengers. Wickes stepped back into the road, and his companion turned the corner; and at once, as in response to a signal, two or three men—unmistakably police in plain clothes—appeared from adjoining corners and collected at the door of the hoarding.

The door was fastened with a padlock. One of the men lifted this padlock, peeped into it, and then looked inquiringly at Wickes, who nodded. This done, the man gave a gentle rap at the door and straightway produced something from his pocket, applied it to the lock and opened it instantly.

"Not strictly regular, perhaps," Wickes remarked to Crook, who was now close behind him; "but we mustn't be over-ceremonious in a case like this."

The ground was waste, and choked with bricks and rubbish. The house was fairly sound, though plainly it had not been inhabited for many years. The ground next the side-street was bounded, not by a hoarding, but by a fairly high wall, and a short covered way led from the rear part of the house to this wall—evidently to a door which Wickes's companion had gone to guard.

Wickes ascended the half-dozen steps and rapped smartly at the front door of the house. There was no response. Wickes beckoned and pointed, and the man who had opened the padlock now came forward and broke a pane in the window of a small room close by the door, inserted his arm, unfastened the catch, and with a good deal of trouble, for it was long since the window had been opened, succeeded at last in forcing up the sash. This done he climbed in, and presently, with a deal of creaking and wrenching and pulling, and much shuddering opposition from the old woodwork, the door stood open.

"Look out there!" Wickes said quietly, with a glance at his assistants waiting in the open. And at once, followed by Crook and Merrick, he entered the house.

In the hall they paused a moment to listen. There was not a sound of any sort. They went a few steps further, and listened again. Still not a sound. Wickes started up the stairs, followed by the others.

"If they've commonsense," he observed, "they'll be upstairs in the daytime for the sake of the look-out—if they're here at all, of course."

It grew plain either that the quarry had no commonsense or were not in the house; for room after room was entered, and room after room had nothing for the eye but dust and grime; nothing for the ear but the sound of the searchers' own footsteps.

"Somebody has been here," observed Wickes—"and lately. You notice that feet have disturbed the dust a little in every room. But I fancy we're too late. If they were below they must have made a bolt before this, and my fellows would have had them. But we'll see."

Downstairs they went, to the kitchen floor; and here evidence was clear that the house had been tenanted recently. For crumbs littered the floor, and sheets of newspaper were spread, one at each end of the room, and on one of these lay a broken part of a loaf, still quite fresh.

"See there," observed Wickes, "somebody has been sitting on each of these sheets of newspaper with his heels drawn up in front of him—see the marks? And the sheets are at opposite ends of the room, too! Now, Mr. Crook, you know about Indian manners and customs. What does that suggest to you?"

"Mehta Singh and Jatterji!" replied Crook promptly. "Mehta Singh would never sit to eat with Jatterji; even when they were not eating he would make Jatterji keep the lower end of the room. These fellows might show themselves very civil to each other before Europeans; but leave them alone, even in such an awkward situation as this, and the pride of race asserts itself at once."

But it was plain, whatever might have been, that neither Mehta Singh nor Jatterji were now on the pre-

mises, nor anybody else beyond the searchers. The
front door had not been opened lately—that was plain
enough—and the grimy windows were fast in their
frames, even as the one had been through which Wickes's
man had entered. There remained the back-door into
Rook Street, and an examination showed that that had
been used, apparently, for both entrance and exit. The
thick dust in the passage in the short covered way was
trodden with footmarks in both directions, and the lock
of the door into the street had lately been oiled.

"We've drawn blank," said Wickes at last, "but
they've been here, for certain. They've eaten nothing
but bread—an Englishman would have brought in more
than that, to say nothing of beer. Tramps wouldn't
have troubled to put down newspaper to sit on, and
Englishmen wouldn't have sat at opposite ends of the
room. They've gone now, anyhow; and the next thing
is to find how they got here. They've come with a key.
We must find out how they got it."

They turned back once more, and took a final look
at the kitchen, Wickes and Crook narrowly examining
every corner in search of further traces. In the drawer
of the dresser they found another loaf, cut in two for

convenience of stowage, but otherwise untouched, and wrapped in a piece of clean white muslin cloth; and by its side lay a bottle, less than half-full of water. Clearly the fugitives had been making no luxurious picnic.

As they turned to leave the kitchen again, Crook perceived, in a dark angle behind the door, what at first he took to be a scrap of white paper. He reached and turned it over, and so found it to be only a similar piece of similar muslin cloth to that in which the bread was wrapped. Something seemed to be in it, and as he pulled it toward him by a corner of the muslin that something rolled out. And it was a green stone—a brilliant green stone, an oval cut stone an inch and a half long!

"Look! look at that!" cried Crook, springing to his feet with the jewel extended in his hand. "Look! In this muslin! On the floor!"

"Gee-willikins!" cried Mr. Merrick, mouth and eyes at their widest. "The Green Eye of Goona!"

All three men stood aghast, and even the stolid lock-breaking policeman was startled out of his habitual serenity, and exhibited signs of lively interest in the discovery.

"I think I must take charge of that," Wickes said presently. "It must go to the Yard as soon as possible."

"Why on earth should they leave it behind them?" asked Merrick.

Wickes shook his head. "Impossible to guess," he said. "No matter how much of a sudden bolt they may have made, this would be easy enough to carry. And more than that, I should have expected one of them to keep it somewhere securely about him, not to leave it lying anywhere loose on the floor like this. But that we shall find out—perhaps. This is satisfactory enough as far as it goes, but what we want is to put our hands on the men. This is merely lost property—immensely valuable, no doubt, but not what we started after."

The discovery was so wholly unaccountable that Wickes at once began another complete search through the house, including cellars, cupboards, outhouses, and every possible place wherein a man might hide. It seemed incredible that the stone should have been left thus. But their second search ended even as the first. Not a living thing beside themselves was in that house or about it.

And so they left the derelict house, perplexed and bewildered. The place was made fast again, and the men were put unobtrusively on the watch once more; for, since the jewel had been left behind, it seemed all the more likely that the fugitives would return to the place to recover it. A few inquiries in the neighbourhood revealed the fact that the site had been bought by the local authority for a block of new offices, and an inquiry at the present offices of that body led to the further information that a local housebreaker had contracted to erect the hoarding and leave the site clear in a month.

It was not far from midday when at length the housebreaker was found—a large, smudgy, and now rather anxious and apologetic person. He hoped there wouldn't be any trouble over it, he protested anxiously. He had the place in hand for the next month, and as long as he got cleared in time he didn't think there'd be any harm in making an extra few pounds out of the loan of the key to a gentleman—leastways, he seemed a gentleman, quite a gentleman. Reassured as to his own immunity from serious tribulation in the matter, the housebreaker was communicative enough. A gentleman had come to him a few days ago, just as he was going off after finishing the hoarding. The gentleman was well-dressed and civil, and said he was the agent of a firm of hide merchants who were changing their warehouse, and wanted a place for a fortnight or so in which to stow a few bales till the new premises were ready. He was ready to pay five pounds down, if he could be given the key for the two weeks, and the housebreaker had seen no harm in closing with the bargain. There would be plenty of time to do his wrecking after the bales had been taken away, and five pounds made a handsome addition to his profit. The gentleman had not had the key of the hoarding, but the key of the door in the side wall; and that was all that the housebreaking contractor could say.

In reply to other questions, it appeared that the gentleman had called himself Mr. Turner, though, as nearly as the man could describe him, he would seem to have borne an uncommon resemblance to Hahn. And so at last the housebreaker was let go about his business, to his great relief. Wickes went off to make fresh mysterious arrangements of his own, and Crook and Merrick went off too—to lunch.

II.

Two days passed, and until the afternoon of the second day nothing more was heard from Wickes. Crook had business of his own to attend to, but found time to call once or twice at Scotland Yard—without finding Wickes in. As for Lyman W. Merrick, he passed those two days in hurrying about in hansoms with a wild notion of helping, or at any rate of seeing something of the progress of the adventure, by pure dint of rushing over as much of London as possible between meals. Each evening Crook dined with him and Daisy; and all three were equally puzzled to account for the doings at the old house at Lambeth, more especially on the second evening, for something which Crook had learned from Wickes that afternoon.

The detective called at Crook's hotel soon after four, and wished to know, first, if he had heard or seen anything of any of the three men they were after, since the visit to Lambeth. Crook had seen none of them, of course, nor heard news; in his turn he asked if Wickes or his men had been more fortunate.

"Well, no," the detective replied; "I can't claim that we have had any very great luck. By the way, you're on the telephone here, aren't you, Mr. Crook?"

"Yes, of course—in the office downstairs."

"Very well. I'll take the number as I leave. Perhaps you'll be good enough to leave a message in the office when you go out, so that we can get in communication with you without any undue waste of time. It's identification I'm thinking about, you know. We're watching the docks and certain other places, and I quite expect one of my fellows will be arresting the wrong Hindoos sooner or later. Of course, we've got the landlady of the house in Redway Street; but she only knows Jatterji, and we haven't anybody at all who knows the others except you."

"Very well. I'll do anything you like, of course."

"Thank you, Mr. Crook. And now see here. Here's the stone you found at the old house." He took the muslin packet from his pocket, unfolded it, and displayed the great green gem. "Here it is. Looks brilliant, doesn't it?"

"Yes, of course it does!"

"Precisely. So it did when we first saw it in that dirty old kitchen. So it did when I had another look at it myself after I left you. So it did all along, in fact, till this afternoon, when I put it beside a real one!"

"A real one?"

"Yes, a real one—at Wetherby's, in Bond Street. This is a coloured crystal, and nothing else!"

"A coloured crystal! Nonsense! Why——"

"If it's nonsense, it's Wetherby's nonsense, Mr. Crook, not mine. But Wetherby's the first man in the trade, and I think you'll allow him to know. He says it's no more a diamond than that window-glass!"

Here was surprise on surprise. Could it mean that Hahn had stolen a mere counterfeit, after all? That all this trouble—these midnight murders, everything—all had been done for a valueless imitation of the real stone? A counterfeit, he knew, had been left behind when first the stone had been taken from the Rajah's tent. But this—how to account for this?

There could be no doubt about it, Wickes insisted. Information of any sort was always worth having in the service, and it struck him that no harm could be done by showing the stone to Wetherby; and Wetherby had declared the thing false at once. More, he put it among other gems of all sorts of colours, sizes, and qualities, and then the fact was made plain to any eye. It was the dullest thing in all Wetherby's shop.

"That's all, Mr. Crook," Wickes concluded, rising briskly. "Of course, all you hear is in strict confidence. And you won't forget about leaving a message in the office when you go out, will you?"

III.

It was on the morning of the next day that another visitor called on Crook at his hotel; a visitor whom he had very little reason to expect.

Crook had finished his breakfast, and had risen

from the table, when a waiter approached and said:

"There's a gentleman asking to see you, sir. Name of Hahn."

"What name?" Crook demanded, astonished and incredulous.

"Hahn, sir. Leastways, that's what it seemed to me."

"Show him up!" Crook replied, as the shortest way of ending the doubt.

Hahn it was, though Hahn vastly altered; a great change from the Hahn who had visited him so short a time ago on his first arrival from Southampton. The man stood a picture of broken nerves and of absolutely grey funk; twenty years older to the view than he had seemed before.

He stood silent till the waiter had gone, and then, plainly with an effort, he spoke.

"I've come," he said, "to make an—an arrangement. Let us settle this matter between us."

"What matter is this?"

Hahn made a faint gesture of impatience.

"We needn't waste time," he said. "You know

what I mean. The green diamond—the Eye. We've
both been after it, and I've got it. But I'm going to
share with you—fairly."

"Have you got it here?"

"No; but I know where it can be got. You can
get it. I'll trust your honour, if you'll give me your
word. And we'll share."

"Why are you willing to share?"

"Simple enough reason. I'm in trouble, and I want
a partner. And so I'll share."

"In trouble with the police?"

"The police? No, of course not. Not the police."

"Then you will be presently. They are after you.
They are after you and Mehta Singh, and Jatterji. For
murder!"

Hahn made another faint sweep of the hand, and
sat down. "That's nothing," he said. "I've made pro-
vision for all that—I can't be touched. So far from it,
indeed, that I half thought of going straight to the
police myself to get out of my trouble; but I prefer to
give you a share, and you shall have it; half of what
we can make of the Green Eye. Come, again I tell you
we mustn't waste time, and to show I mean what I say,

I'll put every card I have on the table, openly. The
diamond came over—you know how, in the Tokay. The
wine was dispersed—never mind about details now.
The magnum with the stone in it went to the old man
Clifton, and he found the diamond when he opened the
bottle. He must have shown it to Pritchard—probably
talked about it—and the result was that Pritchard
killed him to get it. That you know about. Mehta
Singh was with me in the business—that you must have
guessed before this. He got the diamond, though the
contrivance was mine—that and the plan for getting it
to England without risk to ourselves. Mehta Singh
came over with me; but if I could have got the diamond for myself, of course, I would have left him in
the lurch. You remember, don't you, that I offered
to divide with you before—when you told me you
had sold the bottles, and I thought you had the
stone?"

"I do remember, quite well. A very pleasant
scoundrel you are, too, my respectable Hahn, even by
your own showing."

Hahn shook his head and his hand again impatiently. "Never mind about all that," he said.

18*

"Scoundrel, rascal, anything you please. This is business I'm talking; and to put my cards on the table, as I said I would, I must tell you it all. If I could have got the diamond, as I have said, I would have made it my own. But Pritchard got it, and I couldn't find Pritchard. I was following the bottles just as you were, and when I heard of that murder I saw the meaning of it—guessed it, if you like; at any rate, I knew that Pritchard had got the stone. But it was Mehta Singh who found Pritchard—through Jatterji, almost by chance, I believe. He managed to set artful inquiries going in the Indian colony—it's a small one, all in touch together —and he found that this fellow Jatterji was actually lodging in the same house as Pritchard. Well, he told me, and he made his own plans. But just about that time I discovered the whereabouts of another magnum— the one your friend Merrick has—and, as even Mehta Singh had no occasion to waste a murder, he arranged with Jatterji to test the off-chance thus offered as well, before making the definite plunge on what I felt to be the moral certainty of Pritchard. What happened you know well enough. Mehta Singh got the diamond. But I tell you I had nothing to do with Mehta Singh's

crime—I was many miles away at the time—I arranged
to be—and I can prove it. I had nothing to do with
it—planning or execution."

"Nothing except to take the profits?"

"That, of course, if I could get them," replied the
unabashed Hahn. "Why not? Moreover, I have another card to play with the police. Not only was I far
away when the crime was committed, not only did I
have nothing to do with it, but I took steps to have
the murderers arrested; gave the police information,
which again I can prove."

"How prove it? By describing your letter of information?"

"Quite right."

"A note built out of capital letters cut from a
newspaper? In an envelope addressed in the same
way?"

Hahn started slightly.

"Oh, you know it, do you?" he said. "Well, yes
—that was it."

"Hahn, you grow a bigger scoundrel with every
sentence."

"Tut, tut! what does it matter? Mehta Singh had

done his work, and he could be dispensed with; safer out of the way. I am putting my cards on the table, I tell you. There is nobody here but you, and that doesn't matter. You are my partner, or will be—for you'll accept my offer, of course. I arranged for an empty house in which Mehta Singh and Jatterji could hide, and in which they could be taken by the police —after I had got the diamond from Mehta Singh, of course."

"Oh! you did that before you sent your precious printed and pasted letter, then?"

"Of course. That was the proper way, you see."

"And how did you get the diamond?"

"Simple stratagem. You remember that when it originally vanished from the Rajah's tent, a neat imitation took its place? Well, I had had that prepared beforehand. But I had another made also. Mehta Singh didn't know that, but I thought it might prove useful on some later occasion, as it has done. I had a telegram from him while I was away—a telegram can be dropped into a letter-box, you know, at the cost of a little delay, and nobody can identify the sender. Well, I came up and went to the old house at

Lambeth, in the evening, and there, in the dusk, the simplest possible bit of sleight-of-hand did the trick. Mehta Singh produced the diamond, and he thought he got it back; but what he got was the other thing. I left him and sent to the police the little note that you know of. It might have turned out inconvenient, after all, if things had gone well, to have my writing recognised; so I used the printed letters.

"But things didn't go quite as well as they might have done. Mehta Singh must have discovered what had happened very early the next morning. For when I went that morning to Liverpool Street to get my ticket for Holland and to see when my train would start, there were Mehta Singh and Jatterji waiting for me in the booking-office! It must have been Jatterji who advised that move. He would know that Holland would be the place anybody in Europe would make for with a stolen diamond to deal with. He knows European ways thoroughly, and though I believe he's been acting mainly in terror of Mehta Singh all along, he wasn't so frightened as to forget that.

"Well, that was three days ago, Crook—three days ago exactly, now; and from that moment they have never left me, day nor night. They are watching for me now, somewhere outside. Will you send for a drop of brandy, Crook? I am nearly breaking down."

Crook sent for the brandy and watched Hahn take it at a gulp. Then the tale went on. ·

"I wouldn't go back to where I was staying," Hahn said, "because the stone is there—hidden. I had no luggage with me when I went to Liverpool Street, and I believe that is why I haven't been murdered yet. Mehta Singh wants to get me with all my movables together so as to be sure of getting the stone. I know where the diamond is, but it's death for me to get it. Crook, it has been awful! Three days and nights I have been dogged and watched everywhere, and I don't believe they've slept once—I haven't, though I've taken beds at lodging-houses, just as I stand. I've tried all sorts of dodges — hansoms, offices with doors at the back, everything — but they've stuck to me through it all, and now I feel about run down; and, besides, the money I had about me is nearly gone. So I've made up my mind to sacrifice half, and to take you for partner; so my misfortune's your luck. As I said, I half thought of going to the police, seeing how safe I've made myself, but I don't want to risk their turning over everything where I'm staying, and, perhaps, coming on the diamond. That would need a deal of explanation, you see. So on the whole, I'm going to let you have half, and we'll do it like this, and put Mehta Singh safely into the hands of the police at the same time. First of all, I'll remain here while you go off to where I've been staying, and get the diamond. See?"

"Look here, Mr. Hahn," said Crook, standing before him with his hands in his pockets; "I think I've heard about enough of your confidences, and I don't want any more. I'll make no such arrangement as you seem to expect."

"What? Won't you? What? Not take half? How much do you want, then?"

"I want none at all, incomprehensible as it may seem to you. You may——"

"But it's straight, I tell you! Really it's straight! You shall hold the stone yourself all the time—I'll trust you, if you don't trust me. We'll go to Holland together, and——"

"No, no, we won't," Crook interrupted. "I'll have nothing to do with the business, I tell you; not if you give me the whole diamond twice over. Now, see here. You've come here and made yourself my guest, though you weren't asked, and you've made me your confidant, though I didn't want that either. But as it stands, you've taken me into your confidence, and though you are a repulsively foul rascal, I shan't betray that confidence of my own motion. Understand, I'll have nothing whatever to do with you or the diamond you have stolen, and I recommend you strongly to go to the police before they come to you. Now, here's your choice. Come voluntarily to the nearest police station with me, in which case I will pledge myself to do nothing but see you safely there, and leave you to tell your own tale; or sit where you are, and I will send for the police and have you arrested—you and your Indian friends together. Now which will you do?"

Hahn was astonished, wholly lacking comprehension of any man who would refuse such an offer as he had made. But he understood well enough that Crook meant what he said, and presently, after a sullen pause, he rose heavily.

"Very well," he said. "If that's how you put it, I'll come. I'm safe enough, anyway, and I simply go with information of those two fellows."

They went downstairs together, and at the door Crook hailed a distant cab. But now Hahn, standing moodily and suspiciously by his side, changed his mind.

"I won't go with you," he said. "Why should I? I'll go my own way; you go yours."

He turned away, but instantly Crook sprang after him and seized his arm.

"No," Crook said, "that's not so easily done. You know my conditions. Porter, bring that policeman!"

Hahn made the beginnings of a feeble struggle; but the policeman from the corner reached the spot in a few strides, and Hahn struggled no more.

"This man is Hahn," said Crook; "wanted in connection with the Redway Street murder. You know the name, don't you?"

The constable had read the name in the *Police Gazette* only that morning, and he scented credit for an important arrest. "You'd best come quiet," he said, "and remember anything you say will——"

The man never finished the sentence. Crook felt a violent drive at his side, and as he recovered, he turned and saw Hahn fall forward groaning in the policeman's arms; and even as he fell Mehta Singh stabbed again twice, with lightning strokes, under the left arm.

Then Mehta Singh, hatless, eyes and nostrils wide with rage, flung down his long knife and stepped back. Crook ran at him and seized him with both hands. At the clasp the Indian gave one angry wrench and then stood still. "All right," he said, "all right!" with the short, clipped accent of a foreigner who has learned a phrase or two by ear alone. And, as he spoke, his disengaged hand passed across his lips twice, forward and back. But he made no other sign.

People came running, and more policemen. Hahn was stretched, pale and dripping, on the pavement, and a doctor was dragged hurriedly from within the hotel. The doctor ripped open the prostrate man's waistcoat and called for wet cloths; but he looked up at the policeman and shook his head. For lung and heart were pierced, and Hahn lay dying.

Mehta Singh, pushed to and fro between two policemen, swung unresistingly, and slowly grew pale and sweaty. His legs failed, and before a four-wheeled cab could come, he, too, was laid on the paving-stones. And then Crook, at first puzzled, remembered how the Indian's hand had passed twice across his lips, forward and back. And at once it struck Crook that he should have known that a man of his race would almost certainly have made preparation to forestall the ignominy of death by hanging. Which, in fact, Mehta Singh had done most effectually; for both he and his victim were carried away dead.

Jatterji was not to be seen, either then or later. He had fled, doubtless, at the first sign of Mehta Singh's attack. That attack was not difficult to understand. Mehta Singh had dogged Hahn for three days, and now he saw his prey, diamond and all, on the point of being snatched from his grasp by arrest. He had lost the diamond, but he could still take his revenge; and he took it.

It cost Sergeant Wickes some little trouble, and it

took some little time, to discover Hahn's late lodgings.
They were found at last, however—in a quiet turning
out of Baker Street. He had called himself Turner
there also, it appeared. But at that point Wickes's
success came to a singularly complete stop; for not
one trace of the Green Eye of Goona was he able to
discover either in Hahn's luggage or about the house.

Where Hahn had actually hidden that extraordinary
gem: whether or not it still lies there: or if not, who
has it: are mysteries as yet wholly unpenetrated. Certainly not for lack of search in the house near Baker
Street, for indeed that respectable structure was almost
pulled to pieces by Wickes's energetic assistants. But
hidden or lost, found or not, nobody knows where now
lies the Green Eye, and the Rajah of Goona still lacks
the pride of his treasure-house.

Mr. Merrick was among those who were most
energetic in the search for the lost jewel, and I believe
he still harbours designs of buying up the entire
street in which Hahn's lodgings stood, pulling it down,
and analysing every brick. Be that as it may, it is
certain that his immediate excitement at the time was
interrupted by a serious interview with Harvey Crook

on a matter wholly unconnected with the Green Eye of Goona; and that the interview ended in a perfectly satisfactory manner, and earned Lyman W. Merrick several kisses from his daughter Daisy.

After which Mr. Merrick turned to Harvey Crook, and said, "Well, my boy, there's that last magnum of Tokay lying in the middle of my biggest trunk, and it seems to me that this is about the right occasion to open it!"

THE END.

Trieste

Trieste Publishing has a massive catalogue of classic book titles. Our aim is to provide readers with the highest quality reproductions of fiction and non-fiction literature that has stood the test of time. The many thousands of books in our collection have been sourced from libraries and private collections around the world.

The titles that Trieste Publishing has chosen to be part of the collection have been scanned to simulate the original. Our readers see the books the same way that their first readers did decades or a hundred or more years ago. Books from that period are often spoiled by imperfections that did not exist in the original. Imperfections could be in the form of blurred text, photographs, or missing pages. It is highly unlikely that this would occur with one of our books. Our extensive quality control ensures that the readers of Trieste Publishing's books will be delighted with their purchase. Our staff has thoroughly reviewed every page of all the books in the collection, repairing, or if necessary, rejecting titles that are not of the highest quality. This process ensures that the reader of one of Trieste Publishing's titles receives a volume that faithfully reproduces the original, and to the maximum degree possible, gives them the experience of owning the original work.

We pride ourselves on not only creating a pathway to an extensive reservoir of books of the finest quality, but also providing value to every one of our readers. Generally, Trieste books are purchased singly - on demand, however they may also be purchased in bulk. Readers interested in bulk purchases are invited to contact us directly to enquire about our tailored bulk rates. Email: customerservice@triestepublishing.com

You May Also Like

Persecution and Tolerance: Being the Hulsean Lectures Preached Before the University of Cambridge in 1893-4

Mandell Creighton

ISBN: 9780649669356
Paperback: 164 pages
Dimensions: 6.14 x 0.35 x 9.21 inches
Language: eng

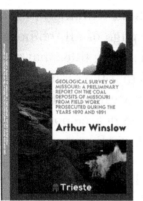

Geological Survey of Missouri: A Preliminary Report on the Coal Deposits of Missouri from Field Work Prosecuted During the Years 1890 and 1891

Arthur Winslow

ISBN: 9780649691807
Paperback: 244 pages
Dimensions: 6.14 x 0.51 x 9.21 inches
Language: eng

You May Also Like

ISBN: 9780649724185
Paperback: 130 pages
Dimensions: 6.14 x 0.28 x 9.21 inches
Language: eng

Report of the Second Annual Meeting of the Maryland State Bar Association, Held at Ocean City, Maryland, July 28-29, 1897

Conway W. Sams

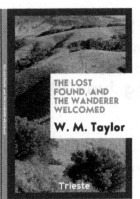

ISBN: 9780649639663
Paperback: 188 pages
Dimensions: 6.14 x 0.40 x 9.21 inches
Language: eng

The Lost Found, and the Wanderer Welcomed

W. M. Taylor

You May Also Like

1807-1907 The One Hundredth Anniversary of the incorporation of the Town of Arlington Massachusetts

Various

ISBN: 9780649420544
Paperback: 108 pages
Dimensions: 6.14 x 0.22 x 9.21 inches
Language: eng

Biennial report of the Board of State Harbor Commissioners, for the two fiscal years commencing July 1, 1890, and ending June 30, 1892

Various

ISBN: 9780649194292
Paperback: 44 pages
Dimensions: 6.14 x 0.09 x 9.21 inches
Language: eng

www.triestepublishing.com

You May Also Like

ISBN: 9780649199693
Paperback: 48 pages
Dimensions: 6.14 x 0.10 x 9.21 inches
Language: eng

Biennial report of the Board of State Harbor Commissioners for the two fisca years. Commeneing July 1, 1884, and Ending June 30, 1886

Various

ISBN: 9780649196395
Paperback: 44 pages
Dimensions: 6.14 x 0.09 x 9.21 inches
Language: eng

Biennial report of the Board of state commissioners, for the two fiscal years, commencing July 1, 1890, and ending June 30, 1892

Various

Find more of our titles on our website. We have a selection of thousands of titles that will interest you. Please visit

www.triestepublishing.com

Lightning Source UK Ltd.
Milton Keynes UK
UKOW06f0936231017
311488UK00005B/791/P